For My Friends
With Fond Regards
Bill

THE ADVOCATE

William J. O'Shea

Bloomington, IN  Milton Keynes, UK

authorHOUSE™

AuthorHouse™
1663 Liberty Drive, Suite 200
Bloomington, IN 47403
www.authorhouse.com
Phone: 1-800-839-8640

AuthorHouse™ *UK Ltd.*
500 Avebury Boulevard
Central Milton Keynes, MK9 2BE
www.authorhouse.co.uk
Phone: 08001974150

First published by AuthorHouse 6/12/2006

ISBN: 1-4259-2875-7 (sc)

Library of Congress Control Number: 2006905302

*Printed in the United States of America
Bloomington, Indiana*

This book is printed on acid-free paper.

THE ADVOCATE

CHAPTER 1

The sunlit dogwoods and red buds, which were at their peaks, indicated what time of year it was, the best time. Southern Illinois was usually quite a lovely place to live, but spring time was its boom period. The Advocate was enjoying the beautiful day strolling, with direction, but dawdling none the less. Unfortunately, there were only a few moments of normal life left for the Advocate. Only a short time to appreciate the world around.

■ ■ ■

Warren Knoop jumped up and down in sheer frustration. His plan had not worked out well at all. All those eight long years in prison, dreaming, planning, fantasizing and now there was nothing to do but jump.

It was too unfair. He'd planned so carefully, albeit somewhat driven. Same time every day. There had been so many to choose from. It had been so exciting. Cleverly, he had been able to conduct his surveillance from the safety of a shaded window in the house he had recently rented. His timing was honed to perfection. He had masturbated each time, preparing for today, working up his courage, and excitement. He had his kit bag ready for work. Video camera, latex gloves, duct tape, condoms, and the knife. It was all ingenious.

There was no one around, no one had seen a thing. Now the cold wetness in his jeans was just another, very obvious, sign of the failure of his plans and dreams. Jump.

■ ■ ■

The Advocate heard a strange noise. Sort of an anguished cry, followed by another sound that was unfamiliar. The noise came from the rear of the building. The sound drew one to it because it was wrong somehow. There it was again. A grunt now, coming from just around the corner of the little frame house.

The scene behind the house would have signaled a profound turning point in anyone's life. It was no different for the Advocate. A tall man was standing in what seemed to be a pile of red and white garbage, glistening in the sun. He jumped and grunted, the second noise came from what was under his feet. A terrible wet squishing sound.

His back was to the Advocate. On the ground behind him were a pair of child's panties, white, with kitties on them. Next to the panties was a thick bladed Bowie knife, lying in the grass as though it were a gardening tool, left out, that had become stained by weather. The Advocate took the situation in quickly, a nanosecond was twice as long as was needed. The sun reflected off the part of the blade that wasn't covered in blood, into the now different eyes of the Advocate, who stooped to pick it up.

▪ ▪ ▪

Warren was so caught up in feeling sorry for himself that he didn't realize there was anyone there until he saw the tip of the blade poking out of his chest. He stood there for a second, dead, not feeling, not suffering, his only thoughts, before he collapsed onto the body of April Fashe, were for the injustice which had been his life. He had told himself that he wasn't going to let this little girl talk to anyone afterwards. That was what had happened the last time and he had gone to prison for eight years. It was supposed to be different this time. It was all planned so carefully. He had practically decapitated the child, after the excitement had caused the premature failure of his fantasy. It was different this time.

CHAPTER 2

The telephone rang while Diego Santucci was chasing a Cheerio around the bowl. When it persisted, as it always did, he gave up on the cereal and reached for the little box, softly cursing, using a word which he had been trying to cut down on. Not a word exactly, an acronym. Back in 1829, when Sir Robert Peel started the first police force in London, the "Bobbies" couldn't spell all that well so they would use the initials of the crimes when they made out arrest records, creating acronyms for many crimes. One of the charges which they had trouble spelling was when they arrested someone 'For Unlawful Carnal Knowledge'. Santucci used it again when he saw it was the office calling which meant he had better get his golf clubs out of the car.

"What?" He asked none too gently.

"What took you so long to answer, Dago?" said the familiar voice of Frank Wesson.

Santucci didn't say anything. He did not like being answered with a question. Wesson broke the silence first.

"We've got a bad one over in Richview."

"Where the hell is that?" he asked.

"In Washington County," Wesson responded.

"What are you calling me for? How bad could it be?" Santucci didn't want to go, but the cop in him couldn't help but ask.

"The preliminaries are a nightmare. Double homicide, and it looks like two different offenders." Wesson didn't want to repeat what he had heard.

"Come on, Frank, what's the big deal? Two bodies, two offenders, can't you find anyone between here and there that has two pairs of handcuffs?" Santucci thought he might get in a round after all, if he resisted enough.

Frank wasn't just Santucci's commanding officer so he felt bad giving this assignment to his friend. Since the recent elections it seemed Santucci had lost his clout. He'd rubbed a lot of people the wrong way over the years, obviously, because he wasn't the best man for this job but his name came down specifically in this case and it came down fast. It sounded like one mistake could be a career end-er.

"It's all messed up already. The thing only happened a few hours ago and there's a renegade sheriff down there who's giving press conferences already. Anyway, there's been a sexual assault and murder of a six-year-old girl and it looks as though someone came along and killed the perpetrator while he was committing the crime and just walked away, leaving the two bodies lying in a yard."

Santucci tried another tactic, especially after what he had just heard. "A-six-year-old? Frank, you know I hate kids. I don't do cases with kids. Come on, guy," he pleaded.

"Listen, Dago," his voice became softer and a little conspiratorial, "this wasn't my idea, it came from up the line, with your name on it. As fast as lightening. I think they're trying to stink you up a little, see if they can force you out."

Santucci was quiet for a different reason now. He'd had a long career. Some people thought it had been too long. The Department of Law Enforcement, Division of State Police, was supposed to be a non-political organization, as all police departments were supposed to be, but were not.

He was a realist if nothing else. "Okay. Who knows, this might be the one that pushes me out the door." Then he added thoughtfully, "maybe I need a push."

"Look, Diego, I'm sorry about this." Frank could have hidden behind the upper echelon decision but was too good a friend.

"Forget it, Frank, I'm not going anywhere yet." Santucci let him off the hook quickly. "Give me the details. And who is this sheriff? Aren't we processing the crime scene already?"

Santucci listened while Wesson gave him the times and particulars on the incident, not writing it down, he never did. There had been no other statement released other than the comments by the sheriff. The major crime van was on the scene, but you couldn't get a real crime scene technician in front of a camera at gun point.

"Where's our spokesperson, what's his name, Mason?" Santucci had a lot more questions but was in a hurry now. He was dressed already and grabbed an old sport jacket, it might get messy out in the countryside.

"Believe it or not, Mason, and anybody else higher than a corporal is down with the flu or something. I don't know who's in uniform down there that we can put in front of a camera."

"Okay, I'll find someone, other than myself." Wesson knew that was coming. Santucci might look good in front of a camera, but he was still an undercover man at heart.

"I'll call you later; my phone doesn't work in the elevator." He lived on the top floor, as high up as he could get, in the tallest apartment building in Springfield.

CHAPTER 3

Santucci pulled his clubs out of the passenger seat of the Corvette and put them in the trunk of the Caddy. Then he put the top up on the 'Vette. This was no longer a nice day. The engine roared on the first click and he pulled out of the underground garage and headed for the highway. When he was clear on Route 4 he let the 'Vette out a little, feeling for balance at higher speeds. It was, after all, three different cars, three junk titles, cruising at 100 mph. It ran like the Submariner watch he always wore.

He made a mental note to tell Ariano that he liked the car. He had complained about the color, the reddest red he had ever seen, telling Ariano that just because he was half Mexican he didn't have to drive a Mexican's car. The chief mechanic never paid too much attention to what he liked or complained about anyway, he was only the boss.

He had keyed the name Richview into his G.P.S. and the map that came up was easy to follow. The town was just off Interstate 64 near Mt. Vernon. It took him about an hour and a half to reach the interstate and he took it east. He passed up a knot of traffic and let the Corvette out again. It was then that he saw the cruiser behind him with its red and blue 'Mars' lights flashing.

Santucci waved. He had a state police bracket on his license plate and stickers on the car that the trooper should be able to see. He didn't have time to stop. Since he had been in the car he had heard the Washington County Sheriff's interview three times.

The trooper persisted so he pulled into the right lane, but he wasn't going to pull over. The trooper pulled up next to his car and he opened his star case and held it up to the driver's side window so she could see it. This particular trooper was a female.

She shook her head and motioned for him to pull over. Santucci shook his head no and made some other urgent expressions which meant nothing to the trooper. She sped up, apparently thinking that she would force Santucci to pull over. He floored the 'Vette in exasperation and pulled away from the cruiser as though it were standing still. He knew he had done something stupid and it was confirmed by a glance in the mirror and the sight of the trooper frantically talking into her radio microphone. He pulled over.

He sat there for a few minutes and waited. The trooper was talking, seemingly nonstop into her radio. When he thought enough time had passed he got out of his car.

"Do not exit your vehicle." The loudspeaker on the cruiser boomed.

Santucci held his credentials out in front of him and continued to walk towards the car, hands in clear view. The trooper said something into her radio again and got out of the cruiser, drew her weapon and stood behind the car door in a combat position.

"Stop!" she shouted. "Turn around and walk backwards with your hands behind you."

Santucci had had about enough of playing cops and robbers.

"My name is Lt. Diego Santucci. Have you ever heard of me?" The look on her face said yes, but she wasn't talking for the moment "I'm ordering you to get back in your cruiser and follow me to Richview. Do you know where that is?" She knew but wasn't saying.

Santucci turned back towards his vehicle. "I said stop!" She wasn't giving up.

"You heard me." Santucci shouted, raising his voice over the noise of the traffic on the interstate. "If you're going to shoot me, I'd appreciate it if you'd try to miss any vital organs. I'd rather you were just fired instead of put in jail."

"You are in violation of felonious traffic laws. You are under arrest. I am in uniform and I am ordering you to submit to arrest." She was still on her game but some of the fire had gone out.

He turned and bowed. "I respectfully refuse." Santucci jumped into the Corvette and pulled away smoking his tires and didn't look back until he was over 100 mph. There she was behind him, lights flashing, trying to keep up.

Twenty miles down the road his phone rang and he cut in the hands free microphone. It was Frank Wesson.

"What the hell are you doing? There's a trooper calling for help on the interstate. Screaming about you to anybody that will listen."

"Calm down, Frank, I just found our new spokesperson," Santucci said, as he slowed to pay attention to two things at once. The trooper was a few car lengths behind him but hadn't tried to overtake.

Wesson laughed in spite of himself. "You crazy half-breed bastard."

"I was a preemie, Frank."

"Yeah, right."

"You're welcome to call me off this case. You can chew me out around a steak dinner on me." Maybe it wasn't too late to get out of this.

"How I'd love to but, no way, *José*. Just remember that they're adding all this shit up, *Amigo*, putting it on your account." Wesson was worried about Santucci, they'd been friends since the academy, after which

Santucci had gone undercover for five years, running a chop shop in East St. Louis, with Frank his only contact with the outside world.

The G.P.S. beeped when he was two miles from the exit, Route 51. He had been watching an uncountable flock of geese heading north, snow geese mostly it seemed, the sun reflecting from their white feathers. They streamed in and out of formation, flying V's. Being raised on the narrow streets of Chicago he never tired of looking at the skies above southern Illinois.

The trooper was right behind him now. He had slowed to 80 mph while daydreaming. As soon as he was eastbound on Route. 51, he looked around and realized that he no longer needed a map. The telescoping TV satellite booms were waving over the crime scene and could be seen for miles. There were no buildings taller than a tree, and the antennas were taller than all the trees.

He was attacked by the media at his car door and had to push his way to a spot just outside the yellow caution tape where he turned to the cameras. The female trooper was right behind him. She was no little thing. She was taller than Santucci, but then a lot of people were, and she didn't have an ounce of fat on her either. She looked the part to him, spit polished. Pretty, but not so pretty that it would distract from the job he had in mind for her. Most impressively, her Smokey Bear hat was tilted at a perfect angle.

"Ladies and gentleman," he said over the twenty questions he was asked at the same time and around the tape recorders and microphones that were fencing to skewer his mouth.

"This is Trooper..ah," he looked at her name plate quickly, "Marzulo." "Marzulo," he said again softly, approvingly, this time to her. "She is the new spokesperson for the Illinois State Police for this investigation. From now on she will be the only person who will be in possession of any accurate information. Now if you will let us check in with the major crime investigators, Trooper Marzulo will have a statement for you soon." He gave them his most charming smile. "Thank you all for your patience." He turned to the trooper so he was out of camera shot, and winked.

Marzulo handled herself well, he had to admit. She announced she would be back to speak to them in a moment and followed Santucci.

"Mister Santucci," she said when they were out of hearing, purposely not addressing him by his rank of lieutenant. Her voice was not at all friendly. "You are still under arrest. I don't care who you are or who you know. You were driving over 100 miles per hour." There, she had said it. Nobody pushed her around.

"Marzulo, do you want the job or not?" He wasn't looking forward to what he was about to see.

"Is this all a fancy charade to avoid the traffic penalties or do you really want me to be a spokesperson for the ISP?" She was coming around.

"Yes." He kept walking toward the tented area. Marzulo made that exasperated noise that her kids made when they were offered no choice, and regretted it immediately.

"Listen....Trooper, what's your first name?" He thought he should work on her being a friend and spokesperson rather than an arresting officer.

"Marine." It was a statement as well as a name. Here come the usual comments, she thought.

"Born on November 10th?" he asked casually.

Marzulo was floored; no one had ever guessed before. Her father was a Marine and when she was born on the birthday of the Marine Corps, she had gotten the name meant for the boy child he was hoping for.

"Why, yes. They call me Marnie though." She knew about Santucci. He had dated every eligible woman from Springfield to Chicago, and she had also heard that every one of them was willing to go out with him again whenever he asked. He wasn't her type, but he was getting interesting.

"Marnie sounds better." He had a very charming smile. Perfect white teeth that matched the white temples of his hair, the rest of which was dark and neatly trimmed. "Be the spokesperson. It won't hurt you any. Don't you get tired of doing the same job every day?"

It was as though he knew what she was thinking. Maybe she had been such a stickler out on the interstate because she was just plain tired of it and was taking it out on everyone she stopped.

"This is going to be a tough job," he continued, knowing the answer, too. "Tag along. Milo and Kozlowski will give you the lines and all you have to do is look official, which you already do. Okay?"

"All right, I'll give it a try," she relented. "But you're still under arrest." She had a nice smile too.

CHAPTER 4

Before he could get to the tent, Milo Kratochvil came up and filled in some more blanks. The crime scene was behind a little white house that was being rented by the dead man, Warren Knoop. He had been released from the Big Muddy Correctional Penitentiary twenty seven days ago, and had not registered as a sexual predator yet, way past the ten day limit of the law. The child, April Fashe, lived down the street and walked to school every day, alone.

When the sheriff's deputies had gone to the child's home, they had found the mother smoking methamphetamine, a drug that Santucci knew was ravaging the entire Midwest. The mother was under arrest in the sheriff's office at the county seat, Nashville, Illinois, and was being moved to the local hospital for testing and sedation.

"Okay, Milo, I guess that's our next destination; now what's the prelim?" Santucci motioned toward the tent, asking for impressions as well as facts.

"They say that the bodies weren't touched, but I'm not sure." Milo was of Bohemian ancestry but not of recent immigrants. Italians, Balkans, anybody who could fit down a small hole had migrated to this coal country early in the previous century. They had come to help dig out the 300 year supply of fossil fuels that lay under the rolling grasslands and hills. When the EPA decided the coal was too dirty to burn, the children of the coal miners had to adapt. It was tough. There were a lot of poor people in the Heartland.

"The adult male was lying atop the dead child, with a 12-inch Bowie knife plunged into his back. Probably cut the bottom of his heart off. He didn't suffer any."

"That's a shame." Santucci meant it.

"We went through the house, not much in there. It looks as though he was watching the children walking to school every day. Had a little box set in front of a hole in the front window shade. The school is on the next block. He was all set for a party-- video camera, rubber gloves, condoms, duct tape. Son of a bitch. I'd like to wake him up and kill him again." Santucci grunted agreement, Marzulo was wishing she had stayed on the highway.

"Today was *the* day, for him at least." Milo and Jim Kozlowski had been on the major case squad for ten years and their impressions were usually right on. "He either snatched or lured her back here. Maybe scared her quiet with that big Bowie knife. He took her panties off, but we don't know what else he did to her at this time because of the condition of her body. There was no rape, we think. His pants were open but that may be as far as he got. Looks like there's semen in his shorts. The child's head was nearly severed and most of the blood was forced out of her when he jumped up and down on her body, in frustration probably."

"Where are the victims?" Santucci hated referring to Knoop as a victim, but that's what he was, at least at this point. He didn't expect the bodies to be on the scene after so many hours. Milo and Kozlowski didn't really need him for that kind of coordination.

"On the way to forensics for autopsy. We left the knife in his back, bagged the handle." Milo didn't have to say that they would go over the handle for evidence of who had held it; Santucci knew this team was thorough.

"Who found them?"

"The little girl had a case worker who was alerted when she didn't show up for school."

"Where's she at?" Santucci was killing time, avoiding the tent. Hell, his specialty was white collar theft, organized crime, a lot of things that came before this.

"*He*, is at the sheriff's office getting the same treatment as the kid's mother probably."

"Was he checked out? Did you go over him?" Of course the person who discovered the bodies was now a most important person, if not *the* person.

"The Sheriff of Washington County, A.J. Gilbert, thinks he's calling the shots and took the guy out of here before we arrived." Milo knew how that would affect Santucci, the same way it affected him.

"We're going to have to talk with him soon." Milo didn't know which guy Santucci was referring to but either one was fine with him.

Santucci steeled himself, quit beating around the bush, and headed towards the tent, Marzulo following quietly behind.

Santucci stopped and gestured to Marzulo. "Milo, this is Marnie. She is our new spokesperson. Give her some lines and some pointers about how to deal with the media while I take a look inside." Milo was relieved; he didn't want to go on camera and Marzulo was also relieved; she didn't want to go into that tent.

There were flood lights at every angle, because even though the sun was shining brightly, it only came from one direction. The digital markers were scattered about in a seemingly haphazard way, each one marking an important point in the topography. Cameras manned by technicians were clicking constantly. With digital photography there was no film to develop and no end to the numbers of photos that could be collected. Even though the bodies were gone, there was a lot of evidence to catalogue. The little girl's panties were there on the lawn, several digital markers around them. There was a *Kitty* book bag with its contents strewn about. Every depression and contour in the ground was digitized.

The blood was dark and coagulated now, looking like used motor oil spilled on the ground. There were smells too: blood, feces, and vomit, mingled together and fought to assault the senses. Kozlowski just nodded his gray head toward Santucci when he caught his eye.

"This ground is soft, Koz. I want three dimensional images of all the prints, and models made as soon as you can." Kozlowski was good at his job. He knew that Santucci was just talking to have something to do besides picture the crime in his head. There would be plenty of time for that.

"And get impressions of every shoe that's been on anyone who has been near the bodies." Kozlowski knew that was coming, and it was a tall order.   The major crime scene personnel were all wearing medical covers on their shoes which would also become part of the body of evidence. The sheriff, the caseworker, and whoever else were a different matter.

"We've got it all covered, Lieutenant." Master Sergeant Kozlowski was an old friend but used Santucci's rank in front of the lower ranked technicians. Jim and Diego were both from Chicago originally, which had immediately given them a sort of comradeship out here in the Heartland.

"Thank you, Sergeant." Santucci picked up on it. The technicians were acting busy. One young man had red eyes, so did another. It would be easy to get emotional at a scene such as this; he wondered who had been responsible for the vomit. It sure wasn't Milo or Jim. They were thick-skinned veterans of this kind of atrocity, meaning that their feelings couldn't get out, not that the scenes of malevolent deeds committed by monsters couldn't get in.

"What are you doing here anyway?" Kozlowski stepped toward Santucci backing him out of the tented area, where he shouldn't be without gloves and shoe covers. Kozlowski used the excuse to light a cigarette. He was tall and thin, and to Santucci, gray in color from all the nicotine he had ingested over the years.

"Somebody up there doesn't like me." Koz knew when he pointed over his shoulder Santucci was aiming toward Springfield.

"Anything for me to do?" Santucci was looking to get a little farther away from the smells and thoughts that came with them.

Raising his voice a little in a kidding way, Kozlowski said, "There's a hole in the wall that we left for you, Lieutenant." He gestured at the opening of a crawl space that was in the rear of the little house.

Santucci gave Kozlowski a wry grin and walked toward the building; he wasn't going to show how he felt about dark holes in the ground. Kozlowski put his cigarette butt in with the ashes in a little box that he always carried for that purpose and stepped back under the rain slicker.

"What was that about?" asked Cardwell, one of the technicians, regarding Kozlowski's little joke.

"He used to be a tunnel rat in Nam. He's always been deathly afraid of dark holes. Lives in a penthouse. He wouldn't go into that crawl space if it was filled with gold." Kozlowski was a little sorry that he had kidded his friend as he watched Santucci bend and look hesitatingly into the darkness.

"Tunnel rat? Viet Nam?" Cardwell was inviting additional explanation.

These kids didn't know a damn thing, so Kozlowski got off the personal subjects. "Get those disks ready. He'll want copies of them as soon as possible. And don't miss a thing. He won't."

"What's he doing here anyway? I thought that he was in trouble for being involved in chop-shops or the mafia or something." This kid wasn't taking the hint. It was none of his business. All he knew about Santucci was the locker room talk. He didn't know a damn thing about anything.

"I'll tell you something that's true about that guy. Santucci showed up at a corned beef and cabbage fund raiser that we had for a trooper's little boy who had cancer. The hat was passed around and when it came back there was a cashier's check in it for the full amount of the money that the parents owed. It was never proved who put the check in that hat, but I know that Santucci was the only guy in the room with that kind of cash." Kozlowski was getting a little hot under the lights.

With a clear finality Kozlowski said, "Now get those disks ready." He started cataloguing the completed evidence bags to get his mind back to work. This was a crime scene, damn it, not a kindergarten class.

▪　▪　▪

The hole was dark. Santucci could smell the cold wet earth. He swallowed hard and shivered involuntarily. It was always cold underground. The daylight only cast a triangle of light on the muddy ground under the house, the rest was black. These old houses were built on a cement block frame with a dirt floor crawl space. They were always cold and wet, and dark. Sometimes, if they didn't have a storm shelter dug into the ground in the backyard, people would crawl under the house during a tornado scare.

If there was a tornado, and this was the season for them, Santucci wasn't hiding in any hole. He was going to jump in a car and become a storm chaser. Although in his case it would be someone who was chased by the storm. He didn't fight with intangibles. He knew that Kozlowski was only pulling his leg. They must have already checked out this crawl space, but he wanted to test himself a little, to see if the fear was still there. It was. For a second it seemed that he could sense something in the darkness, an old feeling was activated.

He heard the screams a split second after his PAD signaled an incoming message. He jumped and smacked the back of his head against the top of the frame of the opening. Backing out and rubbing it, he just stayed bent over for a second to clear his head. That was when he noticed the grass under the faucet for the garden hose was wet.

The screams and the sound of a car alarm were coming from the direction of the street in front of the house where he had left his car. A glance at his PAD confirmed it. As everybody ran towards the screams, Santucci cursed Ariano quietly to himself, again.

It was his car all right. When he got to where he could see it, there was a person sticking out of the window, legs flailing. Marzulo was trying to extricate the person by screwing the legs around and getting nowhere. The window was holding its catch tight.

Santucci fumbled with the remote on his keys and finally got the siren to shut up. The window was going down when he reached the car. The young man that Marzulo pulled out of the window was a squirrelly looking kid with a bunch of 'Press' identification cards on a lanyard hanging around his neck He was in more than a little pain. He was holding his ribs while Marzulo gave him a quick patdown. He had no weapons, although he was holding a computer disk tightly in his hand. She turned his wrist in an unnatural way and the disk dropped into her other hand. She held it out to Santucci and he shook his head; it wasn't his.

"Who are you and what were you doing in my car?" The question was clear enough.

"I, I, I, I...." He sounded like a CD with a scratch.

"Trooper, do you think you could fix that skip?" Marzulo had the kid firmly by the collar and gave him a little shake to get his attention.

That worked. "I didn't know it was your car. I thought it belonged to one of the producers. I was looking for the director's computer. I didn't know it was your car. I'm just a journalism student at SIU. I, I, I'm a, I'm a." The crap was flowing like water, then he got stuck again. "That's my disk!"

"Lock him up for attempted felony theft, and gross stupidity, Officer." Marzulo had cuffs on him and was dragging him, protesting all the way, to her cruiser where she thrust him, none too gently, into the cage in the rear seat and slammed the door on his comments.

They had drawn all attention away from the homicide now.

"That's a dangerous vehicle," she commented when she returned to the 'Vette. Santucci was closing his laptop and putting it back into its leather carrying case. The journalism student apparently had thought that the way to get ahead was to break into cars and laptops.

Ariano had put the motion alarm sensors and automatic devices on the thing. The G.P.S. was nice but most of the other stuff was a pain in the ass. It called him every time the wind blew too hard, and he couldn't figure out how to turn it all off. He spared another bad thought for his cousin, chief mechanic and troublemaker.

"Only to people we don't like." He tried to cover his embarrassment. The media people had been filming the entire incident and were gathering around to gang up on the brutal police officers. "Marnie, handle these people, please. And if they behave themselves and cooperate with you, let the kid go."

"That's two arrests I've lost today." She turned to the throng while Santucci made his way back across the caution tape lines. She was having an interesting day, that was for sure.

CHAPTER 5

The offices of the Southern Illinois Division of the Department of Children and Family Services looked more like a playground or a toy box, than an office where serious business was conducted, but the business was very serious. The toys, and the attempt at a playful setting, were just for the kids.

Nobody cared if they were understaffed by budget cuts (children didn't vote) and a flu epidemic; the place was more chaotic than usual, everyone demanding something at the same time. Sue Rushmore, a tough old bird with salt and pepper hair, soup bowl cut, was overwhelmed at the front desk. Children were everywhere. Appointments were backed up. She handled it well, but was devoid of her usual smiling personality.

"I want to see Miss Akin and I want to see her right now. My little girl is possibly being molested at this very moment and nobody is doing a thing about it. Let me tell you Miss...Rushmore, I'm ready to start doing something if DCFS doesn't start doing their jobs." His voice was deep and booming; he had a low brow, with crew cut hair, close to the skin around the sides. He looked like a cop, or a soldier-- a big one.

Sue Rushmore was no mouse though. "Mr. Crocker, *Dr.* Akin is with someone and will see you next. You can see that it is very busy. Please control yourself and be patient." Rushmore wasn't afraid of this guy, or any one, when she was behind this desk. She'd put more than a few Bozos out, one time even calling the cops and having a parent arrested.

"Patient! While my little girl is being attacked by a sexual predator? Your daughter doesn't have gonorrhea in her eyes, mine does."

Children were abused on a daily basis. Sue knew better than most what evil lurked in the world, but you could only do things one at a time.

The door behind Sue opened and a woman came out weeping, with three mixed race children in tow. She had some forms clutched in her hand. The children were quiet and reserved; they were always that way when they were homeless. Sue knew they would be in the shelter again tonight. At least these children had one parent, however inept she might be at her job. The state of foster homes was dire down here these days with the meth epidemic pouring kids into the system every time another meth cook house was busted by the drug enforcement agents.

"Mrs. Jacobson, I'm sorry that's all we can do for you at this time. Please call the number on the card I gave you to set up the evaluation for Kyle, Jr. When we get the results we can recommend some treatment." The woman who had followed Mrs. Jacobson out of the office was Dr. Angela Akin, now best noted for being the only person who wasn't home sick with the flu. Even though she had an athletic figure and was obviously fit, anyone who saw her, whether they had met her before or not, could tell that she was tired and upset.

"Miss Akin, I want to know why Delbert McKinney is not under arrest and in jail under lock and key." Mr. Crocker had come to the head of the line.

Dr. Akin was tired but had a few brain cells still working. "I would like to know why you are $1,800.00 behind in child support payments." If he wanted to have it out in the hallway, that was fine. "I explained to you over the phone that the sheriff's office is attempting to find Delbert McKinney. They should be looking for you too as far as I'm concerned. Is there any real reason why you have deprived your daughter of her court ordered support for six months, Mister Crocker?"

"My little girl is being victimized by that pervert and you want to talk about money?" He wasn't backing down either.

"Among other things, yes. If you could have been depended upon all along to support the child, maybe your ex-wife wouldn't have ended up with that guy." That was the wrong thing to say and she knew it the minute she said it. She wasn't thinking straight. You couldn't call back words, or deeds.

"She'll go with anyone who can cook meth, you know that. And you know what she will do with any money that I give her." He was right. But it was a way for her to dodge a situation she had no control over at the moment.

"Okay, Jack," she used his first name to deflect him a bit, "I agree with you about Misty's problems, but she hasn't failed a drug test since she was ordered into counseling by Judge Lewis and..."

He interrupted her with as much sarcasm as he could sneer at her. "Meth doesn't stay in your system, Miss Akin, you should know that." He wasn't deflected or softening much.

She'd had it. "You want to know what's going on in the case? You want unsupervised visitations with your daughter? If you want to be more involved in Amy's life, as you say, then fulfill your commitment. Until then, Sue, Mr. Crocker is leaving and will be back with $1800.00...and not until then." She turned and went back into her office and closed the door.

Sue Rushmore didn't know whether to dial 911 right away or wait until Crocker broke down the door to Doctor Akin's office, which he looked very much as though he was ready to do. Then he apparently was able to calm himself and turned and left the office. It wasn't until then that Sue noticed how that exchange had quieted all the other chaotic behavior going on in the waiting room. It wouldn't last long.

CHAPTER 6

"What are you doing with a car like this? Having an end-of-life crisis?" Milo was crammed in the passenger seat of the 'Vette.

"No, Ariano put it together and thinks it will sell easier if I drive it around. Interested?" he asked questioningly.

"Me? Are you nuts? I can't even fit in this thing." Milo was 6'3" and weighed 250 pounds.

"How about Emil?" Emil was Milo's 18-year-old son. "Make a nice graduation present."

"One thing I do agree with you on....this is an old man's car." Santucci shut up.

When they got off the interstate at the Nashville exit, it became obvious that there was an election next week. The sides of the highway were lined with campaign signs, mostly for A.J. Gilbert for sheriff and Tom Donovan for states attorney. "Is that our sheriff?" He asked Milo.

"Diego, this guy is a pip. Wait till you see him. I couldn't figure out if he was for real or not."

"What do you mean by that?" Santucci asked.

"Just wait, I don't want to spoil it for you. I want you to get the full effect just like I did. If it wasn't for that crime scene I would have thought this guy came out of a movie. Hell, he may have."

It wasn't hard to find the sheriff's office. There were dozens of television towers sticking up over the tops of the houses and businesses in the downtown area. They had definitely grown in number. As they came into view Santucci saw vans from St. Louis and Memphis. All networks were represented.

He looked in his mirror for Marzulo's cruiser. She sure wasn't escorting any red Corvette down the highway and she apparently wasn't even getting in sight of one.

Santucci pulled up in front of the post office. They locked the car and he took his laptop. The courthouse was besieged by, among others, KSTL, KLOV, WSPK and WMPS, the K's from the west side of the Mississippi River, the W's from the east. Each news station had staked a claim to part of the lawn that ringed the building so they could shoot with the courthouse in the background. Little islands of people mostly dressed like cultural refugees except for one 'on camera' person who was dressed in business attire. Santucci and Milo slowed to listen to one of the live network reporters. The most professional looking crew was fronted by a small Afro-American woman, pretty, but with a no-nonsense attitude, wearing an expensive suit and obviously not from around here, but then neither was Santucci.

"......sources tell us that Noel Carlton is being charged with the murder of Warren Knoop. It is believed that he came upon Knoop while he was raping and murdering little April Fashe and Carlton then killed Knoop. We have Leonard Harris, our chief legal correspondent, on the line now. Leonard, is this man a hero or a murderer, or both?"

They walked by and headed up the stairs of the courthouse. They were recognized and swarmed by the media for a minute until Santucci pointed out the welcome sight of Marzulo's cruiser coming to a stop in front of the building.

"Who's Noel Carlton?" Santucci asked when they had cleared the sheriff's deputies stationed at the door.

"He's the volunteer social worker that found the bodies. A retired elementary school principal."

"What's this Gilbert's strategy? Whoever smells it first is the guy who cut the cheese?"

"Sounds like it." Milo just shook his head in agreement with Santucci. This didn't look good. They followed the arrows to the sheriff's office.

"The sheriff is busy." This from a deputy who was so overweight that his under shirt bulged out between the buttons of his uniform shirt. After making this announcement, he went back to polishing off a bag of Crunchie Cheetos, licking the cheese off his fingers between mouthfuls. Santucci watched this for a few moments then walked past the desk, telling the deputy not to bother getting up, and into the office.

The sheriff was standing in front of a full length mirror that had a sign across the top reading 'Appearance Commands Respect'. He was well over six feet tall, trim, with a steel gray helmet for a head of hair over a deeply lined face. He wore a brown uniform with gold piping all over the place. He had 'Five Star General' insignia on his collars, a gold badge and plenty of ribbons and medals on his chest. He wore a Sam Browne belt supporting a tooled holster and a gold-plated six gun. A pair of ostrich skin boots and the Stetson hat hanging on a wall hook finished the ensemble.

Sheriff Gilbert aimed his comb at the two menacingly. "I told you people that there would be no exclusive interviews, now........Oh." He recognized Milo Kratochvil.

"Yeah, nice job on the crime scene, boys. We've got it cleared up already though. Why don't you guys clean up and take off?" He acted as though he was doing them a favor.

Santucci wasn't fazed. "I'm Lt. Santucci from the major crimes division. I'd like to have a few words with your prisoner, please."

"Hell, which one? I got a house full of 'em." The sheriff had a practiced political laugh which he used freely.

"The one you're charging with murder." Santucci wasn't laughing.

"Hell, I should be giving Noel Carlton a medal for sticking that scumbag, Knoop."

"Now that you mention it, what evidence brought you to the conclusion that he had killed Knoop?"

Gilbert wasn't sure that he had mentioned anything, and what was the other thing? "Oh, well, before you guys arrived at the scene, I (one of his deputies, Clifford Cox, actually) noticed that there had been some water run out of the garden faucet over on the back of the house. Well, Carlton stated to one of my officers (same sharp kid) that he had not gone near the bodies, but we did a field test on his hands and found blood under his fingernails."

The sheriff was very proud of himself feeling that he had done the state's job, and better. Santucci glanced at Milo who returned a knowing smirk. At least Milo was enjoying himself. Santucci thought they had better get busy before this guy destroyed any more evidence.

"I'd like to see the prisoner," he said, short and sharp. If Gilbert asked which one again, all bets were off.

"Well, okay." Maybe this guy wasn't all facade. "Harris, bring up Carlton so these guys from ISP can talk to him." The fat desk man had been standing in the doorway the entire time, seen but not heard. You couldn't hardly miss him. He got his bulk turned in the doorway and headed down the hallway.

When Harris brought Noel Carlton into the little room he asked if they wanted him cuffed to the metal ring that had been appended to the wall of the old janitor's closet.

"No, that's fine, Deputy." Santucci indicated a chair and the man sank into it. He was in his 60s. He was wearing an orange jumpsuit with rubber shower shoes.

Santucci took one look at the little man, with the bald head and sparse comb over, and knew that he didn't do it. "Mr. Carlton, have they advised you of your constitutional rights?"

"What? Oh yes." The man was unfocused.

"Would you like to speak with an attorney, Mr. Carlton?" Santucci wasn't in a hurry.

"No, I don't need an attorney." The frail looking man was starting to at least pay attention to his surroundings, looking up at Santucci and Kratochvil when he spoke.

"If you feel that at any time you would like to seek the advise of counsel, Mr. Carlton, you have only to say so and we will stop the interview and immediately make arrangements, okay?" The man just nodded, but his eyes were clearer.

"All right then, let's just talk a bit. Tell me anything you'd like to about what happened in Richview. Start anywhere you'd like." Santucci relaxed, sat back and crossed his legs, trying to put Carlton at ease.

Carlton took a deep breath and held it while he thought about where to start. "I got a call from the school and went over to the house to see if Glenda, that's April's mother, had overslept." When he said the child's name the pain of it caused a pause in his speech.

"I couldn't get an answer at the house, but even if Glenda was zonked out, the kids would still wake up when I knocked, so I figured that April had left for school. I followed their usual route; the school is on the next block, but they weren't there." He had been hurrying up the account, but he stopped just as fast. The thoughts that came next were too difficult to express.

Santucci used the interval to give Milo some instructions and give Carlton a moment to compose himself. "Milo, go find his clothes and confiscate them. And see what else they have collected and take possession of it. Tell them that you want to catalogue the stuff, tell them whatever it takes, and then have Marzulo put it all in her trunk."

When they were alone, Santucci pulled his chair up closer to Carlton and said softly, "Tell me."

Carlton took another lung full of air and held it until it came rushing out with the story. "I'm the

CASA for April Fashe," he said matter-of-factly, but stalled again at the mention of the child.

Santucci asked a question to give him more time. "CASA?"

"What? Yes, I'm a CASA volunteer. That's Court Appointed Special Advocate." He decoded the acronym automatically. "We are assigned by the court to a child, or children, that come into the court system. We sort of work for the judges making sure that kids don't slip through the cracks. Most of the time our children are abused or neglected, though with the meth problem, the kids are taken from the home immediately when there's a raid, regardless of their condition. It's considered endangerment, which it is. There are dangerous chemicals and fumes in these home labs." He realized he was stalling and got another breath so he could continue.

"I don't know how I found the bodies. I just had a feeling. It's only a few doors down from their house and.....I just went back there." He was wringing his hands looking down at the floor.

Santucci asked a diverting question to give him some breathing space. "Did you see anyone else while searching?"

"I spoke to a few people, asking after April, but," he was thinking clearly now, knowing what Santucci was looking for. He looked straight at Santucci and said definitely, "I didn't see anyone who might have done it. The people I talked to were residents of the neighborhood."

Let's get to it then, Santucci thought, this guy wants to know who did it as much as I do. "The sheriff is charging you with the killing of Knoop. He says that you told one of his deputies that you didn't go near the bodies. Now he says that you had blood under your fingernails." Santucci left the end dangling.

It was clear in Noel Carlton's mind. Vivid, in fact. Santucci waited.

"Ahhh" Carlton spat, dismissing the charges. "I wish I had killed him. Maybe that's why I told them that I hadn't touched anything. It was so horrible and frightening at the same time."

Big gulp of air now, the thoughts were becoming vivid again. "I did have blood on my hands, though," he said finally, his voice cracking, "April's blood."

Carlton started to break down. Sobbing out the words, he said, "She was lying there with that monster on top of her."

"Her tiny little face was pushed into the mud, the bloody mud. I couldn't leave her like that. I couldn't. I tried to move her. He was so big. I got her face out of the mud...I was going to...wanted to...I don't know... then I realized that she wasn't really there any longer. So I got up and went and washed her blood....." He broke completely, "....She was my responsibility...I was supposed to protect her...it was my job...and look what happened." He laid his head on the desk and let it all go. He didn't care if he was charged with a hundred murders. He had failed his mission. He had failed his child.

CHAPTER 7

When Milo came back Santucci was wiping his eyes and blowing his nose. Milo asked Carlton if he would agree to a polygraph examination, to divert attention away from the obvious, and Carlton said he would.

"Just hang on for a little while Mr. Carlton," Santucci added to try and put the man at ease. "You'll have to stay in custody here until we can get the examiner to test you. I think that after that we can get you released, on a personal recognizance bond if nothing else. We probably couldn't get you out of here right now without exposing you to a lot of unnecessary media frenzy anyway." They didn't have to tell him to wait for someone to take him back to his cell. He wasn't going anywhere.

"Hundred to one he didn't do it," Milo offered.

"No bet." Santucci was ready to get in his car, drive back to Springfield and retire. Milo had two kids in school, one going to college. He wasn't retiring, and somebody had killed Warren Knoop, that was a fact. "Kozlowski said that there's a message on Knoop's voice mail from his new parole officer informing him that he hadn't registered as a sex offender as required. Seems that he wasn't meeting any of the requirements. Big surprise. He made some calls, we're checking on them."

Milo was flipping pages in a little spiral note book. "There was an 800 call made to DCFS indicating that Warren Knoop was a sex offender and his house was too close to the school. We'll have to find out who made that call to DCFS. They were supposed to send someone out but the field investigator had the flu. The point on that was he hadn't registered yet, so how did the caller know he was a sex offender?" Milo and Santucci were in the hallway outside the Sheriff's Office.

"Knoop's voice mail? The guy just got out of prison and he has voice mail?" Santucci tried to keep up with all the latest innovations but there was just too much of it, or maybe he couldn't keep up any longer. He put the thought out of his mind; there was no giving up.

"You can buy a digital phone in the checkout line at Wal-Mart. All you have to do is put money on it at the cash register and it's activated. Of course, you get voice mail. And they deduct generously from your up front money for you to use the phone or any of the features. Then, when the money runs out, so does the phone service. Now you have to put more money on the phone, and you have to go back to Wal-Mart to do that, etcetera, etcetera." Milo made a circular motion with his finger showing the wheels going round and round.

"We want to talk to that parole officer soon, huh?" Milo nodded, jotting the note down. Santucci was the guy who was supposed to remember everything. Actually, Santucci only remembered things until he had time to write them down. A necessary skill when you are an undercover operative.

"Oh, Diego, about the shoe prints." He put out his hand to stop Santucci from opening the door to the office. "I don't think we'll have any problems with the deputies, and certainly not Carlton, I already have his shoes, but there were some deep impressions of a heel that might match those fancy boots that the sheriff is wearing." This was one of the things that made Milo glad he wasn't the ranking officer on the case.

"Milo, go get Marzulo. I want a uniform with us if we're going to get rough with the sheriff." Milo was happy to avoid going into the sheriff's office and headed in the other direction.

Nothing had changed at the front. Santucci walked right past the beached whale at the desk, jerked his thumb in the direction of the interview room to indicate that the prisoner was ready to go back and entered the inner office, knocking as he opened the door, so as not to sustain any comb wounds.

"Sheriff Gilbert. Just to be sure, I think we ought to put Carlton on the liebox. Don't you agree?" He didn't give Gilbert any time to think or talk. "He said he would take one. At this point, I guess that he'd agree to just about anything." He tried to mock the sheriff's laugh.

The sheriff laughed a little but was too busy weighing the circumstances to get into it. "Well, I guess that might be prudent."

"Yes, prudent." Santucci had bad news for this guy.

"Sheriff, there are some deep heel marks in the area of the bodies, so we'd like to get an impression of your boots." He didn't wait for a comment. "You were the first officer on the scene, weren't you." Not a question.

"Uh, yes. But another car pulled up right after me. I wasn't in the area of the bodies." Santucci went on with what he was interested in, "Where was Carlton when you first saw him?"

"Carlton was running down the street when I found him." Gilbert wasn't sure what he was agreeing to.

"Was he running away? Did he see your car and run away?" Santucci didn't like playing word games with this politician.

"He was running down the street, away from me." Gilbert was being vague now that the questions were being specific.

"And you pulled up next to him and he came over to your car." Santucci volunteered.

"Well, he knew that he couldn't get away from me."

"And he then told you about the bodies in the backyard." Santucci knew the answers if Gilbert wasn't willing to give them.

"That's when he gave the excuse that he had found them like that. You see, he was already forming his alibi. Talking about how he had gone to the school and just had a feeling they were back there. Oh, sure. Like I'm gonna fall for that crock." The sheriff was willing to believe just what suited his purposes.

"Nevertheless. We'll interview the neighbors and school personnel, and considering how he performs on the polygraph...you may have to adjust the situation. Knoop's murder may be deemed justifiable anyway."

"Justifiable?" The sheriff wasn't liking any of the words that Santucci was using.

"Sometimes called a 'crime of passion'." The sheriff wasn't smiling any longer.

Marzulo and Kratochvil knocked and were admitted by Santucci. Milo had an evidence bag for the sheriff's boots. He took the lead.

"A.J., we'll be very careful with your boots, we need impressions of all..." He offered the bag.

"You know, I've had it with you ISP assholes. What's your girlfriend for, she fight your battles?" Gilbert did his laugh again and gestured toward Marzulo, who wasn't smiling and was only a few inches shorter than the sheriff.

"Your investigation is over. Now take your bag and beat it. You ain't gettin no boots and you ain't gettin any further cooperation from the county." He said it as though he *was* the county. "You think you can push us around out here? This is my jurisdiction. I was real nice to you boys and look how you return the favor. Now, if you'll excuse me, I have to get ready to address the media." The sheriff glanced toward the mirror to check his stature which was impressive, he was sure.

Santucci's voice became even more calm than usual. It was clear and icy. "Sheriff Gilbert, we want your boots. They are evidence in a murder investigation. This uniformed officer is here to collect the boots."

Marzulo stepped toward the sheriff and the fool grabbed for his gun, unsnapping the holster and trying to pull it. This wasn't the old west and he wasn't very fast. She skipped, sort of, and came down on the top of his instep with her heavy work boots, sliding down his foot to the toes with the momentum and all the force she was able to muster in one step.

It was enough. The sheriff let out a yell that sounded like a roaring bull. He went down and grabbed his foot. Marzulo calmly stepped over him and relieved him of the gold six shooter, and tossed it on the table. Harris had made it to the door by this time and Milo shushed him with his finger to his lips. Harris didn't want any part of what he saw in the office.

Meanwhile, Marzulo had grabbed the sheriff's boot and deftly pulled it off his foot. When she reached for the heel of the one he was holding he kicked out at her and she stomped on his bootless foot causing him to yell again, and yet again, when she yanked off the other boot.

Santucci continued talking as if nothing had happened. "Now A.J., we're going to leave. Take good care of Mr. Carlton. You and I both know he didn't kill Warren Knoop."

When he spoke now, he looked at the sheriff boring into him. The sheriff stopped moaning to listen; it was real quiet in the room. "You are going to stop using this case to campaign on. Also, you are not to give any press conferences, or information on this case to anyone unless you check with us first. Do you understand me?" He didn't wait for an answer. "If you don't do as I say, I am going to tell the press that you did it. And you can sue me. You can sue the state. You can do any damn thing you want. But I'll guarantee you one thing. After next Tuesday, your opponent will be sitting in that chair." Santucci gestured toward the sheriff's chair, then to the others and they left Harris to help his boss off the floor.

CHAPTER 8

Once they were outside, Milo looked over at Marzulo with new respect. "He does bring out the best in people," he said out loud to no one in particular.

Marzulo didn't comment, but said to Santucci, "Lieutenant, it's been fun playing with you guys all afternoon but I've got two kids who could burn the house down any number of ways arriving home any minute and I've got to end my shift. Budget cuts, no overtime, you know."

"Okay Marnie, go take care of the kids and if you want to continue playing spokesperson, give your number to Milo and let him know when you'll.......hey, you said kids? That's what Noel Carlton said."

"Milo, Carlton said that *the kids* would have woken up when he knocked. How many kids were there?"

"Just the one that I've heard of, Diego."

"Do me a favor; find out about it. I hate to ask you to go back in there Milo but..."

"Oh I don't care. I'd like to see if Marzulo broke his foot anyway."

"Well, I need to get a room and a shower, make some notes, and call Frank to tell him to expect some flack from the county.   I'd like to work out some of this tension too. Is there a gym around here?" Marzulo looked him over before she answered him.

Tension? He didn't look tense or act as though he was stressed out as far as Marzulo could tell. She was still pumping from the little dance she had had with the sheriff. She told him how to get to a club in Mt. Vernon that would honor his gym membership card and what motel was the best.

"Diego, why don't you stay with Polly and me?"

Santucci knew Milo's wife and had met his kids at outings but didn't want to impose and said so.

The news people were milling around not wanting to believe what Marzulo had told them, that there wouldn't be any further news releases tonight, from the state police, or from the sheriff's office.

When he got back to where his car was parked Santucci found the journalism student sitting on it. This kid was young but it had to be common knowledge that even the people who owned them didn't sit on vintage Corvettes.

As he approached, the kid slid off the hood and Santucci grimaced. "Excuse me Lieutenant, sir, could I please have my disk back sir?" He was a big kid, sort of soft looking. He had long hair that was matted into dreadlocks and looked as bad on him as shaved heads looked on white guys. His clothes would have put him right in with any 60's crowd.

"I can see that I made an error in not having you arrested. If that paint is scratched.....oh get the hell out of here and leave me alone will you?" It had been a long day and Santucci was looking forward to getting his mind off of it.

"I'm sorry about the paint, sir." He feigned wiping it with a dirty hand, "but I really have to have that disk. You see, my, uh, homework is on it and it's real important."

"I have about a half a nerve left and you're yanking on it kid." Santucci's voice changed again. There was a time when he was running the chop shop that this guy would have received a very public and intense beating for going near the car in the first place. He had left that person far behind himself and he didn't want to return to doing things the *street* way. Luckily for them both, the kid sensed something and moved out of the way without another word.

The ride to Mt. Vernon was uneventful. He found a room at the Inn and got more directions to the gym. His doctor had given him a choice. Since he was on the verge of high-blood pressure and a few other possibilities, it was medication or daily workouts. Now he hated to miss even one day in the gym.

They were quite pleasant at the front desk. No fatsos here. No problem either. "Please let us know if there's *anything* that we can do for you, Mr. Santucci." He wanted to think that the beautiful blonde meant more than just workout advice, but he wanted to think that all the time, so he went to change and get to work.

The 'I'd rather work out than eat dinner' crowd was pretty heavy but he found a machine that suited him and got to work. After a while a woman, as opposed to the girl at the front desk, got on the elliptical trainer next to his. They competed in an unsaid contest which forced him past his regular pace. He quit before he fell off the machine and tried to get a better look while he toweled off a little.

She was just his size, not taller than he was, and she was very attractive. She was fair, and had short auburn hair that danced when she moved, early 40's maybe. When the feeling came over him he dismissed it knowing how easily he told himself that the woman he had just seen is the most.....that she is the one.

He decided to quit daydreaming and moved to the weight room. After a few minutes she walked into the room. When he looked up and caught her eye he knew that she wasn't interested in him or anything like him. Her eyes were like clouds, blues and grays that swirled with currents. This woman had a mind and she had something on it.

There was a heavy bag and several speed bags suspended from elastic cords, ceiling to floor, in the rear of the room. The redhead pulled out a pair of gloves, red leather mitten types with a finger roll bar in the palm, and proceeded to punish all the bags in the room. Santucci tried to watch surreptitiously but couldn't help staring at her. She punched the heavy bag, then tried to kick it off the hook. Then she worked on the speed bags, one at a time, then two, then three, kicking and punching them away every time they came back at her.

She stopped suddenly and looked straight at him. "You wanna take a picture?" The eyes turned to thunderstorms and bore down on him.

Threatened and embarrassed, Santucci was at a loss for a second, not his usual predicament. "Uh, no, sorry." He stumbled and picked up his towel and started walking away. As an afterthought he said over his shoulder, "A video tape maybe." He didn't stop for an answer, or for a working over such as the heavy bag had received.

CHAPTER 9

Santucci stood under the hot water, trying to wash his brain. He was an old fool. Never married and never really looking. When he finally got waterlogged enough he went to change back into his only clothes. He was going to have to pick up a few personal items. Always in a hurry, here he was, wrong car and no change of clothes. He was glad he always had his gym clothes. His phone had ten missed calls on it. When he picked it up, it rang.

"Diego," it was Milo. "The victim has a brother...... ah.......Michael Fashe. He's nowhere to be found. The sheriff is on a new media quest now, searching all over for the kid. We've got hound dogs, horses, ATVs, I swear, everything's going nuts out here." Milo sounded worried, which worried Santucci even more.

"Where are you right now?" Santucci got the information and was on the highway in three minutes.

The sheriff set up the headquarters for the search in front of the house where the murders had taken place. Since the television crews hadn't all pulled out of the area it was the perfect place to start from, and to campaign from.

"I ain't said nothing about the case," was all the sheriff had to say when Santucci fought his way past the caution tape once again.

"All right, A.J.," Santucci was back to his calm self. "Tell me what's going on."

"Uh...the woman, Glenda Fashe, has two kids. She was supposed to take the girl to school herself, but she was whacked out on meth and the girl went to school by herself. When we asked the mother where the other child was she couldn't tell us anything about the boy. She freaked out about the little girl and they've got her sedated now, but there's a lost little boy out there somewhere." Now that it looked as though the sheriff had dropped the ball and could end up looking bad to his adoring press, he was more than ready to cooperate with the state police.

The entire population of Richview seemed to be up for the event. It was dark now but the floodlights lit up the residential street of the little town. There was a woods behind the row of houses that contained the Fashe home and the one where the murders took place. The howl of bloodhounds and the motors of the all terrain vehicles could be heard coming from the woods. Beams of light could be seen flashing through the trees with their leaves just forming. Milo had mentioned horses, but the only evidence of one Santucci could see was some runover manure in the street.

"Did you search the house?" Santucci couldn't see what good his going into the woods would do.

"Uh......no we didn't." The sheriff didn't know what the hell he was supposed to do but he sure looked good, Santucci thought, although the black shoes didn't go with the ensemble all that well.

A.J. turned to his deputy, "Harris, where's Cox? Get him on the radio and have him to search the kid's house."

"Yes sir." Harris started fumbling with his radio microphone, trying to get the earpiece to stay in his ear at the same time.

He spoke into the microphone, received a response, and said to the sheriff, "Sir, he says that he already searched the house. And now he's searching Knoop's house." He jerked his thumb over his shoulder towards the house they were standing in front of.

Just then they heard the child screaming. They turned for the rear yard as the media overflowed the barricades and came after them. Harris was overwhelmed but made a good account of himself, waving his hands in a vigorous manner and shouting to no avail.

At the back of the house, Santucci and the sheriff found Cox crawling out of the black hole that was the crawl space. "I thought you checked this out." Santucci whispered to Milo who was right behind him.

"We did. There was nothing in there," Milo said helplessly.

The child had stopped screaming now. Cox spoke up hearing the exchange between the two. "Excuse me, sir." He waited for permission to speak. Santucci just looked at him.

"The boy is way up under the house where the dirt goes up to the floor. They probably couldn't see him. I only found him because I heard him whimpering while I was in the house. When I crawled under there and put the light on him, the little guy freaked out. He wouldn't stop screaming until I turned the light off." Cox was standing up now holding his six cell Mag-Lite, which had a powerful beam.

"Hell, just crawl in there and grab him," Gilbert ordered the deputy.

"Sir, he's way in there and won't come out. I can't get up there between the joists to get to him." Cox was as big as the sheriff, bigger in some places.

"Get me a damn chain saw. We'll cut a hole in the floor and just lift him out." The sheriff made a motion as though he was lifting a baby out of a crib. Milo grimaced, picturing what could happen during that scenario.   Then Santucci said something that Milo couldn't believe.

"I'll go get him."   Santucci couldn't believe it either.

"Oh yeah? Yeah. That's a good idea. You go get him Lt. Santucci." The sheriff looked down at Santucci's Italian shoes and did his laugh. Then he glanced over at Cox who was covered in dirt, and smiled.

"Let me hold your coat," the sheriff taunted, but Santucci was past thinking about what the sheriff had to say.

CHAPTER 10

"Diego?" Milo questioned quietly, being the only one on the scene who knew that this was more than a matter of getting dirty for Santucci. "We can get someone else..."

"We don't have time. How long has he been in there?" Santucci threw the question out for anybody who could answer it. Cox knew.

"Probably going on 12 hours, sir." Cox answered Santucci's next question and the lieutenant looked at him with growing approval. "It's about 40 degrees, sir. Here's my light, sir." Cox extended his Mag-Lite to Santucci.

"No light. That's what's scaring him." Santucci knew the false security the darkness offered.

Santucci took off his coat and handed it to the sheriff who kept his agreement momentarily, passing the jacket over to Harris, the official coat holder. Milo reached over and snatched it out of his hand. Santucci was looking at the sheriff.

"A.J., I don't want to see any cameras when I come out." It wasn't a request.

That was okay with A.J. Gilbert, since he saw the possibility of this coming out with Santucci as the hero instead of him. He told Cox to see to it and the young man went to assist the other deputies, who were manning the caution tape with difficulty.

No use putting it off. Santucci crouched down on all fours and scuttled into the hole in the side of the building. Once inside he stopped and tried to reach out with his senses. He knew what to do. He just wasn't sure he could do it. He was breathing too heavily already. He tried to calm his heart which he could now also sense was going faster than it should. He had to keep his mind on the task. He couldn't let it stray back to the tunnels of Viet Nam.

"Michael," he called out softly.

"It's me, Diego." He listened and heard movement off to his left and he turned towards it. Another sound and he turned more to his left and moved toward it slowly.

"I'm from the state police. My name is Diego Santucci, I'm a lieutenant. Are you all right?" He kept talking to cover the sound of his movements. No answer from the boy.

"Everything's okay now, Michael. I'm going to help you. I used to go underground back in the war..... to help people." To help the people above the ground, the ones under the ground were the enemy. The tunnels would contain Viet Cong officers most times, hiding by day and coming out by night to collect taxes and distribute punishment for anyone who helped the Americans. Long rods were used to find the tunnels. Then all you had to do was dig into it, drop in some smoke and try to see where the entrance was. Grenades didn't help much because there were turns in the tunnels to stop the shrapnel and concussion. After all that, the only thing to do was go down there and get them out. That was the *Tunnel Rat's* job.

No sound from the boy. The dirt was going up now and he could sense that he was near the joists of the floor. It was darker than night, black as pitch it might be called. The sound of his voice reflecting back told him that the space was narrowing.

"Don't be afraid, Michael." He didn't know if Michael was afraid. Santucci was telling himself not to be afraid, but it wasn't working. The smell of the earth was strong in his nostrils. It was wet but not muddy. His shoulders scraped against the two-by-twelve boards. He couldn't turn around now. But he couldn't go any farther.

His muscles were fighting him, refusing to respond to commands. He pulled himself forward, not caring about the boy hearing him now. No sound from the boy. Maybe he was in the wrong space. Maybe the boy was between the boards to his right or left. He reached out with his left hand, right shoulder back so he could squeeze further into the space. His heart was racing, blood roared in his ears. Panic started to rise up in him.

The darkness exploded with swirling lights which were only in his eyes. He was blacking out. He was stuck. He wished the sheriff would cut a hole in the floor right this moment.

He could call out. Call for help. Call for help, the way Frankie Cooper had done in Viet Nam. It had been too late for Frankie then; it was too late for him now too. He couldn't even call out. A little cry escaped his lips. Not loud enough for anyone to hear.

He didn't realize that he was trembling until the steady little hand touched his. Actually the hand touched his wrist. Santucci realized that the luminous dial of his watch could be dimly seen in the darkness.

Then he heard the little voice whisper. "Don't be afraid, Diego."

Startled, Santucci tried to swallow what felt like a tennis ball, tried to speak, but his voice was clogged, his throat suddenly as dry as a desert. The touch of the child's hand on his seemed to calm him though. There wasn't anything to be afraid of.

He found his voice. "I'm not afraid Michael........... ....not any more." He admitted to his rescuer.

"Can you crawl to me? We have to get out of here."
He could feel that the boy's hand was cold.

"There's a bad man out there," the boy said, then
he added sadly, "he hurt April."

"He's gone now, Michael."

A whispered secret. "He's the new neighbor; he's
upstairs." Santucci could tell the boy was pointing up
as the hand left his for a moment.

Santucci wasn't sure how much he should tell the
boy, but the little guy had been acting more mature
than he so far. "That wasn't the bad man Michael.
The bad man is dead."

"I was scared and I came in here. He's too big to
get me here." Maybe that's how the boy knew that
Santucci wasn't the bad man. Right now they didn't
have time to discuss it.

"He can't hurt you. I won't let anyone hurt you,
Michael." Santucci said it with as much conviction as
he could muster.

"You promise?" The voice was unsure.

"Michael, I never have to promise. Everything I
say is a promise. I always keep my agreements and I
always tell the truth." He said it and he meant it.

The boy thought about it for a second and then
started crawling toward Santucci without comment.
None was needed.

Santucci now found that he could easily maneuver
himself in the narrow space and retreated with the

boy hand in hand. He could feel the child's breath on his face. When they reached the more open part of the crawl space the hand pulled Santucci to a halt.

"I gotta pee," the boy said as a matter-of-fact.

"Uh, okay." Santucci was faced with a problem that he hadn't considered.

"Go ahead." He realized that he could see the child now. He was wearing pajamas.

"Make sure nobody's watching." He saw the boy gesture towards the opening. He turned away, making sure that nobody was watching, not even him.

When he figured the little guy was done, Santucci called out for a blanket and was given one immediately. He wrapped the now shivering boy in the blanket and passed him through the opening. The bundle was immediately taken from him and he followed it.

"You better be taking that child to an ambulance A.J." Santucci called out to the retreating sheriff.

The sheriff turned back to Santucci's voice, stopping his rush towards the cameras. He had forgotten to have an ambulance on the scene. Hell, he thought, there were some volunteer firefighters who were taking part in the search, they could take a look at the kid. They took the same courses as the EMTs, some of them.

Before A.J. Gilbert realized it Santucci blocked his way. He reached out and took the bundle out of the sheriff's hands. If the sheriff had protested, Santucci thought he might kill the man. He shook the thought out of his mind. Then he called out to Milo who blocked for him until he could get the boy into the Corvette and pull away with him. The cameramen tried in vain to keep up with him on foot, shooting pictures all the way.

CHAPTER 11

Santucci stopped on the next block and used his gym bag to make a booster seat and put the seat belt on Michael. Then he called Milo and found out where the hospital was. Milo agreed to calm the situation at the scene and meet him there.

"Is this your police car?" Michael was fascinated by the multicolored lights and gadgets mounted all over the dash board; so was Santucci. The heater was blowing on high and the boy had stopped shivering.

"No, this is my regular car. How do you feel Michael? Is anything hurting you?" Santucci tried to watch the child and the road at the same time.

"This isn't a regular car, Diego. I never saw a car like this before." As an afterthought he said, "I'm all right."

"Just because you've never seen something before doesn't mean that it doesn't exist, right?" Santucci wasn't sure if what he had said meant anything to the kid, or to him either. He wasn't very good with children.

"Well, okay. I'll learn about everything when I go to school next year." They looked at each other at the same time. Michael had dark hair and large brown eyes that were ringed with long lashes.

Maybe he thought that Santucci didn't believe him because his eyes opened even wider and he spoke as though he was imparting knowledge to another child, "You have to be five to go to school."

"When will you be five, Michael?" Santucci had never been in a conversation with a child. You smiled at them and you said how cute, or whatever, they were, but he had never actually spoken more than a few words to one.

"I don't know exactly. Soon. In the summer, I'll be five. I'm about a quarter to five now," he said seriously.

Santucci choked and coughed, trying to contain the spontaneous laugh that the boy had evoked.

"Are you okay, Diego?" The child felt that he needed to check on his charge when he acted funny.

"I'm fine, Michael." He couldn't contain his smile. The boy smiled back and Santucci couldn't believe what a beautiful sight it was. This kid was something he had never run into before. And he had done a lot of running.

CHAPTER 12

St. John's Hospital was a two story affair which had been cobbled onto for the last 40 years and was now a collage of metal, bricks and glass. Everybody in the emergency room was immediately in love with Michael. He played to his audience and delighted every one. They fed him, cleaned him up and dressed him in hospital pajamas while Santucci tried to clean himself up. Michael checked out fine and insisted that the doctor examine Santucci also, which they made a show of to satisfy the child. He wasn't satisfied.

"You didn't listen to his heart," he told the ER doctor. The doctor quit trying to fool the child and took Santucci's blood pressure and listened to his heart and pronounced him healthy, officially. The nurses resumed fussing over Michael the minute the doctor left.

Milo had shown up in the meantime. "Diego, I've contacted the DCFS on duty supervisor and told her that Polly and I will keep the boy for the night. They don't have any field personnel available due to the flu epidemic, or so they say."

"Will that be okay?" Santucci realized he was becoming overly protective of the boy.

"Sure, we're certified foster parents although we don't foster children any longer." There was a sadness in the big man's voice.

"I never thought of you being the type to take in wayward kids, Milo." Santucci tried to lighten the conversation a bit.

"Apparently, I'm not. When our kids grew up Polly still wanted to raise children, and I figured it wouldn't hurt to help out some kids, so we went through the training and certification. The first few times they brought kids to us it was fine. Then they brought us a newborn baby girl that had been taken from the mother when she gave birth and tested positive for drugs. She was a crack baby and the little thing just trembled all the time." He was looking past Santucci now, recalling bitter sweet memories.

"We had to hold her day and night for a week. Couldn't put her down, even for a second. Then, after we got her through the withdrawals, it was always something else-- doctor visits, therapy; we were pretty busy. You couldn't help but fall in love with her, though. Prettiest thing you ever saw." He didn't say her name, it was too painful, but he smiled a bit.

"We raised that child for three years. And then the mother wanted her back. She had cleaned up her drug habit, as far as the courts and DCFS could tell, and they ordered us to give her up." Santucci could tell that Milo was deeply affected by the experience.

The big man sniffed and cleared his voice. "I'll tell you something, Diego, I wouldn't cry if *I* died, but I cried when that car drove out our driveway with that child." Another sniff. "So I told Polly no more. I couldn't take that again. So she became a CASA Volunteer."

"CASA? That the organization that Noel Carlton belongs to?" Santucci remembered that interview too clearly.

"Huh? Oh yeah. You see, people can advocate for children in many ways. The fostering was too much for us, well for me anyway, but CASA gives Polly a way to advocate for children and she doesn't bring them home." He tried to laugh a little but it was clearly something that had been hard for him.

"Noel is my CASA, too." Little pitchers had big ears. "He's real nice." Michael was sitting on the examining table listening to every word. Santucci made a mental note. Not the last.

"Where's my mom?" Children often asked questions that grown-ups didn't have answers to. "Can we go see her?"

"Uh.....I'm not sure." Milo answered Santucci's unvoiced inquiry.

"Maybe she's here in the hospital." The little guy wasn't to be taken lightly, they could both see.

"Milo, check on it for me will you?" Milo pulled his cell phone and left the room.

"The hospital would be the right place for my mom, Diego." Then he added in a lower voice, "She smokes. Maybe they could make her stop smoking here."

Sounded logical to Santucci, as did everything the kid said. "Maybe they could." He didn't know what else to say.

"Smoking is hazardous," Michael said as though he were reading the side of a pack of cigarettes, not realizing that his mother smoked different things.

"Uh...yes it is." More words of wisdom from the adult.

"What's *hazardous* Diego?" Santucci marveled at how the child had picked up his name immediately and used his first name so casually, just like old friends.

Santucci tried not to start the answer with 'Uh?'. "A hazard is something that is dangerous. Something that you should stay away from."

"That's right," the child confirmed.

"Why, thank you, Michael." He couldn't help smiling at the boy and was rewarded with one in return. Just then Milo came back and motioned that the woman was upstairs. Michael got it too.

"Can we go and see her?" Michael asked.

Milo was shaking his head but Santucci was learning that it was difficult to deny this child. "Let's see." The kid accepted that.

When they got to the second floor it was obvious which room his mother was in because there was a deputy parked in a chair in front of the door. His name plate said, *Harris,* and he looked as if he could be related to the gigantic desk officer, although he was only half as big.

Santucci identified himself and asked to see Glenda Fashe. The deputy had planned to read his hunting magazine and have a quiet night. Now this.

"Sorry, sir. No one is allowed to see her." He stated very officially. Nobody was seeing this woman. His cousin, A.J. Gilbert, had told him that nobody was allowed in and that was that. He stood in front of the door in a 'you shall not pass' stance. State police didn't mean a thing to him, this was Washington County. A.J. had told him a million times, "We run it in our county".

Santucci decided to get tough right away. "You know about what happened regarding this woman's little girl?" The guard nodded slowly. He wasn't liking the way this was going.

"This is her other child." Santucci gestured toward Michael. "He wants to see his mother." Santucci's voice hardened. "You tell him he can't see his mother, Officer Harris." Your move deputy, he thought.

Harris looked down at Michael. The boy just looked back, waiting for the deputy's response. Nobody could refuse that face.

Harris buckled under the strain. "I.............I've got to call the sheriff to see if you can go in." He practically ran down the hall.

Santucci stepped forward and pushed the door open for him and the boy to enter. Milo wouldn't let them be disturbed. He was sure.

The woman looked too young to have children. She was slight of frame; smoking meth-amphetamine didn't put much weight on. She lay there unmoving, deeply asleep, an IV tube running from a bag to her arm. Michael went right to the bed and took her hand. He held it for a moment, then he reached up and touched her face and lightly brushed her eyelashes.

"She's asleep now, Diego. She'll sleep for a long time, I know." The boy gave his diagnosis. He had treated this patient before. He spoke to her as though she was sitting up smiling at him. "Don't worry, Mom. I'm going to take good care of you."

"This is Diego. He's a policeman. He killed the bad neighbor. He won't hurt anyone anymore." Michael looked up at Santucci who could only nod agreement. He sure wasn't going to contradict this kid while he was talking to an unconscious woman.

The boy took Santucci's hand and led him from the room. "She'll sleep for a long time now, Diego," he repeated.

Outside, Harris was running down the hallway again and Milo had begun to step in his way when the door opened. "It's okay, mister. My mom's asleep. You watch her close, okay? When she wakes up she'll want some cereal."

Harris just stood and stared at the little person with the big orders. Santucci caught his eye and verified the orders for the deputy. Harris stepped aside and prepared to resume his post in front of the door. If A.J. questioned him he planned to deny everything. He wasn't sure what the hell had happened anyway.

Santucci carried the boy outside; it was quicker and more convenient. The child wanted to talk to everyone. "Milo, I guess I will take you up on that offer of a bed for the night. I need to do a little shopping, and I can pick up some clothes and things for the boy."

Milo didn't mention that Santucci was getting attached to the child. But he knew that something unique had happened under that house. Santucci had never showed any concern for anyone who wasn't a female at least close to his age. "Good, Polly and I will need a little time to get things ready anyway. Do you remember the way to my house? It's just off the interstate at Exit 83."

Santucci said he remembered the directions to the house but needed to find a Wal-Mart or someplace similar. Milo gave him directions.

CHAPTER 13

The Wal-Mart in Mt. Vernon was the same as all the rest but Santucci soon learned that he didn't know his way around them very well. Not as well as Michael, that was for sure. In the children's section, a woman noticed him trying to measure the boy for a pair of pants and took pity on Santucci. He bore her comments politely, grateful for the assistance.

"Is this your grandchild? I have twelve grandchildren and two great-grandchildren. My daughter Noreen has four and her little boy Seth is just about the same size as your child." He let her go on sharing grand-parenting tips with him while Michael smiled at the woman, captivating her easily.

Michael gave Santucci a different kind of smile and a little wink when the woman was turned towards the shelf picking out undershirts for the boy. Michael knew Santucci didn't know how to buy children's clothing and had lured this kindly grandmother over for some help. She somehow got the idea that Santucci was taking care of the child during a family problem and stocked the cart as though Michael only had the clothes on his back, which was correct. Santucci just stood there and marveled at the boy. He realized that he couldn't comprehend how this child had grown so old in only four and three quarter years, about.

"He is the most beautiful child I've ever seen," she said, after Michael had slumped onto a pile of clothing that had grown in the shopping cart. She looked around, embarrassed, to see if anyone was listening, "Don't tell my daughters I said that. You know?" Santucci nodded his willingness to keep her confidence and thanked her profusely for her genuine professional assistance.

Even at this late hour, it was past midnight he realized, the checkout lines were few and crowded. He pulled in behind a little blonde girl and her boyfriend. On the right side of the checkout line, just as Milo had said, was a rack with telephones hanging there in clear plastic packages. *Must be activated at the cash register* was the first thing that caught the eye. They apparently wanted to discourage people from stuffing them down their pants, since they wouldn't work unless you paid to have it turned on. *Long Distance, Voice Mail, Just Like a Regular Cell Phone*, was the second thing he read on the insert. What would they think of next? He was too tired to think about it. He reached for one and put in on top of the pile.

"I wish I was in Guam." This came from a grizzled old man who was in line in front of the young couple. He was speaking to the little blonde and she was frozen by the statement.

"You know Guam?" He asked her; the boyfriend didn't know what to say either. The old man was buying three boxed cakes, all the same. Santucci could tell that the old guy was on his last legs. Obviously an alcoholic, the sweet tooth was just one sign, the man stopped the forward progress of the line while he waited for an answer from the girl.

Santucci spoke up and said simply, "Yeah, Guam. Nice place." The old guy refocused on Santucci.

"I wish I was back there." He wasn't moving. "It was better then. Were you in the war?" He hesitated, "Dubba-ya two? You know, the Pearl Harbor War?"

Santucci shook his head, "No, I was in Nam."

"Huh? Oh." Viet Nam didn't mean much to many people.

The old vet went back to the blonde. "I was down in Marion today, at the VA. You see I got two different shoes," he pointed at them. "They want to cut off another part of my foot."

He realized he was holding up the line and turned towards the waiting cashier. "You know, it was better then. Back in Guam."

Out in the parking lot, after more than the minute that was advertised, Santucci had the new car seat and the sleeping child belted in. He then slid onto the highway wondering if the people who made wars had something in store for this little boy that would mark him for the rest of his life.

CHAPTER 14

S antucci was dreaming of a butterfly that floated around his head, gently brushing his cheek with it's soft, flower petal, wings. He opened his eyes and saw Michael, three inches away from his face. He tried not to flinch. In the morning light the little boy still looked as though he had been painted by Da Vinci.

"What's this, Diego?" Michael pointed to a gold medal that Santucci wore around his neck.

"That's St. Michael."

The child laughed delightedly. "That's not right. I've been to church a lot, and I never heard of St. Michael."

"What did we say about things we don't know about? That doesn't mean they don't exist."

The boy conceded the point. "Who was he?"

"He was a warrior who fought a dragon. He's the patron saint of police officers." Santucci was remembering his mother's tales of St. Michael. She had given him that medal after he graduated from the police academy. He wasn't sure why he kept it or why he never took it off. It didn't feel like a spiritual object to him, but it was, he knew, to his mother. She often asked him if he still wore it and he could tell that a *yes* answer made her feel good.

"When did St. Michael live?" The kid had some good questions. There weren't many dragons around here.

"Well, St. Michael never really lived like we do, I guess you'd say. See, he wasn't a man, St. Michael was an angel." He was screwing up this kids head, he was sure, because he was sure he didn't know what the heck he was talking about.

"Oh, I know an angel." Suddenly the boy had it figured out. "Doctor Angel, and she's not a man either. She's a girl."

That was good enough for Santucci. Polly Kratochvil, Milo's still lovely wife, came in, said, "Good Morning", and started giving orders. The two males looked at each other and started hopping. After Santucci had showered and ripped some new underwear out of the plastic he felt pretty good and went looking for a promised cup of coffee while Michael played in the shower.

"Diego, what is all this stuff?" Polly referred to a kitchen table top covered with the proceeds of their wanderings at Wal-Mart the previous evening.

"What?" his voice sort of squeaked non-responsibility for anything bad.

"This game box and all these game cards. This stuff is expensive," she scolded.

"Not as expensive as children's clothing," he countered. "There's one category where size has no bearing. Did you see the shoes? They light up." He liked the shoes as much as Michael had.

She wasn't through by a long shot, though. Milo had come into the kitchen and was quietly enjoying seeing someone else get the logic express for a change. He just sipped coffee and tried not to laugh out loud. "What's this telephone? Surely you didn't buy a telephone for a five- year-old boy?"

"Of course not," he defended sternly, "Milo had mentioned those things while we were working on the case last night, and I thought we should check one out." There, that ought to hold her.

"Check one out? These things are expensive. And you have to put money on them in order to make calls." She smiled finally, an always welcome sight. "Diego, you spend money like a drunken sailor.

"Like a drunken marine." Milo spoke up before he could remember to keep quiet. He got the look.

Santucci bailed him out by blundering again. "After we have finished checking it out, why can't the kid play with it?" Now he got the look. "Dumb question, huh?"

"Forget it Santucci. I don't care if you buy him a car." He smiled sweetly at her.

"You didn't did you? You wouldn't. By the way, where did you get that car?" Milo snorted some coffee. Santucci figured silence was the best approach.

"Oh, there's never a dull moment when you're around, Diego, that's for sure." She had that smile going brightly so his silence was working. Polly was going to enjoy their latest predicament.

She tossed the new phone gently at him. "How much time is on this thing anyway?"

"Just a hundred."

"What! A hundred dollars. Who's he gonna call?" No wonder they were still married. This woman was fun.

She gave in again, partially. "I'll use the thing for whatever comes up regarding the boy." "Now, we've got to go down to the DCFS Office in Marion this morning and have the papers for the temporary placement issued. And they'll probably want to have him evaluated if there's someone there who doesn't have the flu."

There were a lot more orders and plans that followed and Santucci and Milo accepted their roles with humility. The only way that was allowed.

CHAPTER 15

Polly let the boys go to Marion by themselves in the 'Vette. She said that it would take her a while to clean up after them and get ready herself. She dressed Michael in all his new clothes.

While they were at it, Milo filled him in on what had happened overnight. The team was going back in by daylight just to go over everything again, for the umpteenth time. Every neighbor would be interviewed. Video tapes from the local gas stations, mini-marts, everything would be scoured for clues. They were making latex models of the impressions in the soft earth at the crime scene in addition to computer models. Santucci liked redundancy on an investigation. Crimes were not solved by gut feelings or inspiration; they were solved by hard thorough police work.

He already had copies of the digital disks from yesterday. He didn't ask how Milo had come up with the copies so fast, knowing Kozlowski had a hand

in it. The two were like magicians. Still no sign
of the parole officer for Knoop. His office had not
heard from him and had gotten only voice messages
when trying to reach him. Sheriff Gilbert had been
quiet overnight. He had wallowed in the limelight
of the media cameras, taking total credit for saving
the child from certain death. His chances for re-
election, next Tuesday, were certainly alive at the
moment.

In the daylight, Michael was even more impressed
with Santucci's car. He was also starting to get into
the style of the thing, smiling and waving at people
who couldn't help looking their way, as though they
were in a parade.

Santucci slid off the interstate at Exit 54A,
westbound. The G.P.S. beeped when he approached
the light at Route 148. He made the turn and found
the DCFS building among the other similar squat
structures that were across from the airport. He
wanted to carry the boy, still a little too protective,
but you couldn't play with the new shoes if someone
was carrying you. Silly.

Santucci held the door open for the jumping child
and was surprised to see Michael run right in and
up to the counter. "Hi, Rush!" he exclaimed to Sue
Rushmore, to her delight. Michael was apparently
known at DCFS.

"Hi, Michael!" she answered enthusiastically, but Santucci thought he could see sadness behind her eyes. He sure felt it every time he gave it any thought.

Just then the door behind her opened and a woman walked out. "Doctor Angel!" Michael was even more delighted to see her. "See, Diego, I told you I knew an angel."

Santucci couldn't swallow the lump. It was the redhead from the gym. She hid it quickly, but she recognized him. "Michael, how you doin' buddy?" She opened the door and the boy ran into her arms, gave her a hug, and then turned and started searching through the drawers of Sue Rushmore's desk. Apparently this was an old game to them. He soon came up with a favorite flavored sucker, which he also knew what to do with.

"Lt. Santucci?" It wasn't a question. Santucci found a piece of his voice.

"Uh, yes. Polly Kratochvil said she'd call. We're here to..." He didn't have a clue as to what.

"Let's go down to the conference room." She started down the hall. The women weren't *asking* for anything today.

"Michael?" It was a question.

"Michael will be fine. Believe me." Santucci turned to see Michael whispering into Sue Rushmore's ear. She nodded and took the little boy's hand and headed for the bathroom.

"Michael, I saw you on television yesterday when Lt. Santucci rescued you." She smiled down at the little boy.

"No, no," he corrected, as an adult would speak to a child. "I rescued him." Stated as a simple matter of fact. He didn't wait for her reply having other things that needed more explanation. "Rush, you ever heard of St. Michael?"

"Sure." The rest of the conversation dwindled with the two down the hallway.

Santucci and Dr. Akin had stopped in the hall listening to the exchange. The doctor looked at Santucci, waiting for an explanation. Santucci couldn't see her eyes too well in the hallway light, which was good because it made it easier to lie. Without saying a word, he snorted a dismissal of the darned things that kids come up with, shrugged ignorance at the same time and turned towards where he hoped the conference room was.

In the conference room Santucci didn't sit next to Dr. Akin. He told himself he wasn't afraid of her, he just wanted to be able to see her better, from a little farther away, a little more than arm's length.

"I'm sorry about the comment at the gym." Not that. Don't start talking about that. He had been willing to forget about it. He was sort of hoping they'd forget about it.

"I'm sorry, too. I was looking for a place to work out and....ah...I'm not from around here ah..." How lame.

"You sure aren't," she grinned. It wasn't the smile she gave Michael, but it wasn't the thunderstorm look either, that was for sure. Santucci took a breath.

"I recognized that Corvette on the news when you were taking Michael away from the crime scene, the one from the parking lot of the gym. There are definitely not many cars like that around here. Who picked out the color?" The smile broadened into a tooth whitening commercial.

"The color? Oh.....not me....my cousin Ariano did... you see, I'm sort of in the automobile business. When I'm not doing this, I mean." For such a suave guy he was really doing a great dork impression. The stormy eyes from the gym were long gone now. In the calm, they were dark blue in the center lightening to gray at the edges of the iris. He looked down like a school boy, realizing he was staring again.

She read the look and was maybe a little uncomfortable herself, clearing her throat before finding a word that went down a different path. "Michael. He's really a most unusual child.   April was the same way. They deserved better. (Pause) The two of them used to roam the streets of Richview at all hours of the night. You see Michael is small for his age, inadequate nutrition. The mother was strung out on meth and she was indicated for neglect. That's how the children first came into the system last year."

He tried to lighten the obviously sad tone. "Unusual? Last night I took him to Wal-Mart, to pick up a few essential things, and he coaxed a woman into helping us without her realizing anything more than that she was visiting with him and having a good time with us."

Thinking about last night, Santucci realized that he was sort of proud of the boy, and wondered if that was bad. He was sure the doctor would say something if he stepped out of line, unfortunately, assuredly. He tensed and tried to concentrate on what she was saying.

"That's what I meant about him being able to take care of himself. In many ways he is already an adult; these situations bring out strange qualities in children." Her tone changed, slightly, noticeably. "What a shame about April. She was a beautiful, wonderful child. It was really terrible." It was Dr. Akin's turn to detach for a moment. She had to force herself to continue. "He's going to be placed with the Kratochvil's temporarily." She stressed the last word, eliciting a response from Santucci.

"What happens then?" Santucci was on the defensive. "What about the mother? The family?"

"The mother, Glenda Fashe, is a drug addict. She recently passed a series of drug tests, how I don't know, and barely met the minimums for return of the children. Part of the reason the children were returned to her was because the aunt, who had the children, became ill and couldn't care for them any longer. The biological father was killed in prison. There's no other family. Now Glenda will, without doubt, be terminated."

Santucci was concentrating, trying to digest what she was saying, but not happy about the content. He stopped her with a wrinkle of his brow. "Terminated?" He didn't like the sound of it.

"Termination of Parental Rights. Glenda was on the verge of it when her aunt took the children. When the aunt became ill they only returned the children to Glenda because there was no place else for them to go. The foster care system is overwhelmed and she managed to fool the court for a while into believing that she had quit taking drugs. Now she'll be prosecuted for criminal neglect leading to the death of her child, besides the drugs charges which have mandatory sentences attached to them. She was under specific court order to walk the child to school everyday because they lived too close for the school bus to pick her up. She was always shaky, who knows what her mental condition will be after this."

Santucci didn't mention the obvious fact that if the children hadn't been returned to the mother, April would still be alive. From the look on Dr. Akin's face, he didn't have to mention it. He was glad, for them both, when she changed the subject. He was surprised when the subject went so far afield.

"I heard that they are going to charge Noel Carlton for killing that monster," she said.

That was a proper way to categorize him, Santucci thought. He was sorry he couldn't give her any information.

"They haven't charged anyone as far as I know." Lame comments were coming to him easily now.

"They can't charge him. They just can't. I know he couldn't have done it." She was suddenly vehement. "It will hurt the program across the country if he's charged with murder. Even after they prove that he wasn't the one, it will already be too late. The thought that he was involved will always be there."

Santucci knew Carlton couldn't have done it either. He was sorry that he couldn't tell her that he wasn't going to allow any charges to be placed against Carlton.

"Don't worry about it. No one's been charged with anything yet." He repeated it but it didn't seem to satisfy her. It was his turn to change the subject and he asked her what was going to happen with Michael.

Akin filled him in on what was going to happen to Michael in the short term. He would speak with a counselor today, be evaluated, and a program would be designed for him. Santucci duly noted the procedures and agreed to whatever she wanted. He asked only that he be informed of anything that came up regarding the *incident*, as he called it.

He didn't get a yes or no, and just hoped for the best. A person who had the power to *Terminate*, take away another person's right to be a parent, was someone not to be arguing with. He was sorry that he didn't know more about the laws pertaining to juveniles, and decided that he had some reading to do. At this point he was happy that he had some input into what was happening to Michael.

"You'll have someone very good at counseling children?" More protective comments.

"I'm sorry to say that I'm the best that we have."

He didn't know how to take that and wasn't asking for clarification. She got up; apparently the meeting was over because she started towards the front. This was fine because his foot was stuck in his mouth anyway.

CHAPTER 16

When they reached Sue Rushmore's desk, Michael was nowhere in sight, but Santucci's apprehension was easily abated when he heard a familiar squeal of delight come from the area just on the other side of the counter where the children's toys were piled.

Santucci, always looking around as nervous detectives are wont to do, glanced into Dr. Akin's office which was just this side of Rushmore's desk. Sitting in Dr. Akin's office on the visitor's side of the desk was a man. When Angel Akin looked where Santucci was looking she exploded. He'd seen that face before.

"What the...heck are you doing in my office?" She didn't mean *heck*. Akin's shout caused the man to jump up out of the chair. He was more than a head taller than both of them and Santucci perceived that the guy was a threat so he moved into the office ahead of Akin. He glanced around the room, checking out the spaces and possible weapons; he never carried a gun. A laptop computer on her desk caught his eye when whatever was on the screen changed when he looked at. The flat screen now began to flash a series of children's faces, quickly, a couple a second. Apparently it was some kind of screen saver program.

"The door was open and I came in to wait." Sounded like a plausible answer, but not to Dr. Akin.

"There's no waiting in my office." She looked around just as Santucci had done, not seeing anything out of place. She looked at Sue Rushmore who was hovering in the doorway in a distressed condition.

"Ange, I don't know how he got in here. I took Michael to the bathroom and when we came back there was no one around. I had left the outside door open but there was no sound." She looked at the seemingly innocent man as though she would gladly snap his head right off.

"Well, never mind." She dismissed the thing more to ease Sue's discomfort than as an act of forgiveness for the invasion of her office. "What can we do for you, Mr. Crocker? You remember what we said last time you were here?" *We* being the State of Illinois Department of Children and Family Services, all of them.

"Yes, I remember and that's one of the reasons that I came." Crocker looked at Santucci, and his essential Wal-Mart clothes, then over to Akin as if to request privacy. He wasn't getting it at any price.

"This is Lt. Santucci of the ISP." There was no handshaking. Santucci tried to grow a little under the scrutiny of the taller and bigger man, although he hadn't cared much about size since he beat up the biggest kid in school. They eyed each other as wild animals, and people, sometimes do.

Suddenly, recognition dawned on Crocker's face. "I know where I saw you. On television last night. At the double homicide." That was another way of wording it.

Crocker was buddy-buddy all of a sudden. "Well, I'm sorry to say that it wasn't me that killed Knoop. I was in court all morning yesterday, in Saline County, Lieutenant." Santucci wondered why the guy would give himself an alibi in the first minute after they had met. It seemed as though everybody wanted to be the one who did it, but wasn't. Santucci looked over at Akin.

"I was working all day." More alibis. He wasn't interested in who didn't do it. He realized that he wasn't all that interested in who did do it either. Not in the usual way.

Crocker turned back to Dr. Akin. "Here's a postal money order for the entire amount that I owe, plus three months advanced child support." He handed her the check and waited for an apology. He would have had a long wait.

"Fine. Sue can set you up for supervised visitations with Amy." It didn't sound like a big deal to Santucci, but apparently it was.

"Thank you, Doctor." He was very appreciative. Then he gave her a different kind of look, sort of wicked schoolboy look. "I have a present for you, Doctor."

She wasn't biting. Crocker went on with the drama by himself.

"Outside."

He started for the door and Akin followed, which drew Santucci after them. He motioned for Michael to stay where he was after they had exchanged happy smiles. Michael stayed but he knew something was up. There would be questions later.

Outside, Crocker led the way to a four door pickup truck; Santucci could see someone in the back seat. Crocker fumbled with his keys for a moment and the windows started to go down. That action made Santucci realize how hot it was outside and how hot it must be in that black pickup truck.

"Help! Help! Call the police. Help!" The cries came from the rear seat passenger. He was as thin as a concentration camp survivor. He had long stringy hair that was matted with sweat. He was wearing a tee shirt and jeans that were also soaked.

"Shut up, you maggot." The guy shut right up. Crocker waved his hand at the truck as though he had just completed a magic act. "Dr. Akin, may I present Delbert McKinney, fugitive, maggot, child predator, and now your prisoner."

Santucci walked up to the window; Akin had stopped short. McKinney was handcuffed between his legs to a ring that was fixed in the floor. Santucci turned to Crocker. "Just who are you, sir?" Better to start out polite.

"Sorry, Lieutenant, I think that everybody knows me." He started fumbling with his back pocket, drawing out two wallets.

"Do you know Sergeant Major Sanders from District 13? He can vouch for me." Santucci knew him but wasn't talking. Santucci looked down at the impressive array of identification. John C. Crocker, Fugitive Recovery Specialist. Federal Firearms Authorization. Immigration and Naturalization Service Authority to Transport Illegal Aliens. This guy had more ID's than anyone he had ever carded. To Santucci all that translated into just another cop want-to-be.

Santucci had no comment really, but he was sure that Dr. Akin didn't want to deal with the gift that she had just received. "Now who is this guy and why the steam bath?"

"My daughter has the 'clap', or should I be polite and say gonorrhea, in her eyes. And this pervert is the one who gave it to her."

Santucci glanced back at Akin and saw that the guy was telling the truth. Crocker didn't wait for another question.

"The sheriff," he spat out the word, "couldn't locate this individual. That's what I do. So I went and found him and took him for some testing..."

"Testing?" Akin spoke up.

Crocker smiled. "We had a lot of fun getting the slides."

The prisoner whimpered in the back and wailed. "He, he, put rubber gloves on and then he took..........."

"Shut up, maggot!" He shut up.

Crocker smiled at Dr. Akin, gesturing towards his prisoner. "Well, there he is, Doctor, all wrapped up." Crocker was giving him away all right, but not without a parting comment. "I hope the guy that killed Knoop gets this maggot for a cell mate."

All in all Santucci thought that McKinney was pretty lucky, and in a lot better shape than Warren Knoop, considering he had sexually molested Crocker's child. Santucci wasn't so sure he could have shown the restraint that Crocker had. If it had been his child. If he had a child.

He called for a car to take the prisoner to the county lock-up. Best not push it and leave the guy in Crocker's care much longer. He didn't look like he would last much longer in the hot truck with the windows up at any rate.

After the car pulled away with a grateful McKinney, Crocker was given a schedule to visit his little girl, who had been treated and was no longer showing the effects of any diseases. Then he said his good-bys and Santucci was able to visit with Michael for a while longer until Polly got there.

Santucci found it hard to say good-by to Michael and felt that the boy was having trouble, too. "Polly has a phone that you can use whenever you want. She'll set it up with my phone number on speed dial. Then all you have to do is...." Michael looked at him. He knew how to make a phone call. Santucci rubbed the kid's head and held his chin for a last look. Michael jumped into his arms for a last hug. Santucci almost started to cry. He sucked it up.

"Don't worry, Diego, I'll be all right." And Santucci didn't doubt it. And he was less worried.

On the way back to Springfield he caught up on his voice mails and dictated some notes into his laptop using the voice recognition software. At one point he called Milo.

"Keep combing the area. Someone has to have seen something. Make lists of all the names. Find out who was around, who could have been around. Put all the video you collect from the convenient stores on a disk for me. They're going to question Michael without putting any pressure on him. Make sure."

Milo said he would and acknowledged that there was a special interest.

"Milo, do you know a guy named Jack Crocker?"

"Yeah, he's sort of a character. 'Mister Bounty Hunter.' Why?"

"I met him at the DCFS office. He's a character all right. Caught a guy who had sexually molested his kid and brought him to Dr. Akin as a present."

"Doesn't surprise me. I hear he's fairly good at the fugitive recovery. I also hear that there is a lot of money in it."

Santucci had another thought. "Milo, did we ever get a hold of that probation officer?"

"No, but my money is on the sheriff." He could tell that Milo was half kidding.

"How about Crocker? He made a point of telling me he was in Saline County Court all morning yesterday. Do you think we should check it out?"

"It wasn't him, Diego."

He wouldn't doubt Milo but the comment was so matter-of-fact that Santucci waited for more.

Milo caught it and reluctantly explained his reasoning. "He's too tall, Diego. The guy who killed Knoop was short, about your size, no offense." None taken.

CHAPTER 17

When Santucci's cell phone rang he looked at the strange number and almost didn't answer it. It was Michael.

"What are you doing, Diego?" he asked.

"I'm going back up to Springfield and I've been taking some notes and stuff. What have you been doing?"

"Nothing." Santucci could tell that something was wrong.

"How do you feel?" Maybe he should turn around.

"All right." Not so.

"What happened after I left today?" It was like an interview.

"Nothing." A long interview.

"What did you do after I left today?"

"We just talked about stuff."

"And how do you feel about that?"

"Sad." Now we were getting somewhere. Somewhere Santucci didn't necessarily want to go.

"Well, you have those games that we got for you yesterday. You could play with them." No answer.

"You have the phone; you could call someone and talk for as long as you like."

"HELLO!" Oh, right. He was talking with someone.

"Well, where are you right now?"

"I'm at Polly's, watching TV."

"What are you watching?" Might as well try to find something to talk to the kid about for a little while.

"Golf."

Santucci couldn't believe it. "You're watching golf?" Meaning, not cartoons or something childlike.

"I like golf." Michael knew what he meant.

Was there anything he didn't love about this kid? He was beginning to doubt it.

"Why do they "lie," Diego?" For a second Santucci didn't get it.

"Oh, you mean when they say "he's lying two or three?""

"Yeah, why do they lie?"

That launched a conversation that continued all the way to Springfield. Birdies were his favorite, because everyone cheered when you got one. Michael didn't like football. They were too mean. Always hitting.

CHAPTER 18

The phone was ringing in his dream and turned out to be ringing in real life too. Sorry that he had forgotten to turn it off one moment, Santucci grabbed for it the next when he thought that something might have happened to Michael.

Sure enough, it was Milo's number. "Hello," he said a little too excitedly.

"I didn't think you were up yet." Milo's voice wasn't panicky so Santucci relaxed a bit.

"How's Michael?" He hadn't relaxed all the way.

"Fine." Milo had something else on his mind. "Go turn on the television."

"The television? What channel?"

"Any channel. It's all over the media."

"What?"

"I'd rather you got it the same way I did, makes a better impression I think. Call me back." Milo hung up.

Santucci reached over the clock and grabbed the remote for the box in the bedroom. It was only 9:00 a.m., he hadn't slept that long.

The first screen he saw flicked off just as he focused on it, which stirred a screen flicking off memory for a second. Then he realized what the last words he had seen on the ticker were: ....THE ADVOCATE

He started going from one news program to the other waiting for the story to recycle on one of them.

Some of the words scrolling across the bottom of one screen caught his eye. ...I REGRET KNOOP DID NOT SUFFER AS HE HAD MADE THAT INNOCENT CHILD SUFFER. I URGE ALL DECENT PEOPLE TO PROTECT OUR CHILDREN. THE ADVOCATE.

The name of the child predator jumped out at Santucci. He continued to watch and search the channels, putting the PIP on anything that looked promising while surfing the others. Then he had it all at once. "This e-mail was sent to the St. Louis Star and appeared on their front page this morning." The screen lit up with the message and scrolled slowly so that anyone could keep up while the anchor person read it out loud for people who couldn't read:

OPEN LETTER TO LAW ENFORCEMENT: YOU HAVE THE WRONG MAN IN CUSTODY. I AM THE ONE WHO THRUST A KNIFE INTO THAT MONSTER, WARREN KNOOP. I HEARD A

NOISE WHILE WALKING DOWN THAT STREET AND WAS DRAWN TO IT. I AM SORRY THAT I WAS TOO LATE TO PROTECT THAT LITTLE GIRL. BEHIND THAT HOUSE I FOUND KNOOP STANDING ON TOP OF THE CHILD. HE WAS STANDING WITH HIS BACK TO ME. A THICK-BLADED KNIFE LAY IN THE GRASS WHERE HE HAD DROPPED IT AFTER USING IT ON HER. I COULD SEE BLOOD ON IT. CALL IT THE HAND OF PROVIDENCE, A HIGHER POWER, OR WHATEVER YOU LIKE, IT JUST CAME TO ME IN A FLASH. I KNEW WHAT I HAD TO DO. I REGRET KNOOP DID NOT SUFFER AS HE HAD MADE THAT INNOCENT CHILD SUFFER. I URGE ALL DECENT PEOPLE TO PROTECT OUR CHILDREN.   THE ADVOCATE.

Santucci hit the return call button on his phone. "Well?" Milo's voice had a different tone now.

"What do you think?" Milo had obviously had more time to work on it than he did.

"I think it's legit." Milo sounded sure. "Too many references that no one else knew about. In fact it seemed that the person knew they had to supply things that weren't put out to the media."

"Where'd it come from?" Santucci expected more information after being played with.

"E-mailed from a coffee shop in Carbondale." Milo knew a few things. "It's a little student joint. No cameras and terminals all over the place for anyone to use. They have a wireless hookup but whoever it was knew better than to use their own computer. I have some people on the way over there to start working on it."

"Well, I could have thought of a lot better ways to wake up." There wasn't much he could do that wasn't being done, he guessed.

"Sorry, you got company?" Milo realized that the great Santucci had gone a couple of days without female companionship.

"Uh...no." Santucci realized what was on Milo's dirty mind and wondered why it hadn't been on his dirty mind as well.

Santucci changed the subject. "I guess I better get up and get down to headquarters and face the music." Before Milo could say anything Santucci's phone indicated that someone was ringing his doorbell. "Maybe the band is coming to me; I'll get back to you Milo."

He flashed off and cleared his voice before speaking into the phone again. "Who is it?"

"Lt. Santucci, it's Jay Gibbons from Channel 5 news in St. Louis. We'd like to talk to you regarding the message from the Advocate." He gave his name and title as though it were a pass key to any door.

Santucci knew that they were recording the conversation hoping that he would say anything that was airworthy. "Thank you for stopping by,

Mr. Gibbons, but you know that we can't make any comments on investigations that are ongoing. When there is any information to be released the ISP spokesperson will do it."

Gibbons tried to get a word in edgewise or any other way before Santucci hung up, without success. Santucci hoped they wouldn't be waiting to ambush him when he came out, but it didn't matter one way or another. The situation had jumped over the frying pan and gone straight into the fire.

CHAPTER 19

The Advocate was the topic of discussion, period. Even though the staff was at full strength for the first time in weeks, Dr. Akin's staff meeting had been going on for half an hour and they had not accomplished one thing.

"I took the 800 call about Knoop living next to the school." Sue Rushmore had the undivided attention of everyone at the big conference table. "It was a male voice. I told the police that. But I also told them that we didn't have enough field personnel to send anyone out to check on it."

"But why did they want to talk to me so badly?" The police had gone out to Bonnie Weatherlow's house · because she had been off work with the flu.

"Because I assigned you to the case, Bonn. I realize that you weren't at work that day, but it was in your sector." Bonnie had a scary look on her face. Sue hurried on, "Bonn, you said you would be back to work the next day. I'm sorry, I didn't know you would need another day off." Sue wrung a napkin in half trying to explain away her feeling of mismanagement, or of guilt. If someone had gone out to that house....... maybe.

"Well, I was questioned by the police. The state police! They came to my house. Did they go to anyone else's house?" She looked around. The answer was no.

Bonnie was reliving a moment. She had gotten the message Sue had left on her voice mail, but told everyone she hadn't. She also didn't tell the police what she was doing on the morning of the homicide, when she was supposed to be back to work.

"It's not important now, Bonnie, Sue did what I told her to do." Truth or not, Akin just wanted to stop the topic from being discussed any longer. That was the end of it. She wished. Akin's mind was going six ways at once and she was having trouble just keeping it together.

She went through the motions: calling up cases on her laptop, spending a few moments on each one, and assigning new cases that had piled up over the last ten days. They talked about the Coalition Against Sexual Assault Conference coming up in Chicago and complained that they had to provide their own transportation even if their room and board was paid for by the department. Some car pooling was discussed and some excuses for not going were accepted without scrutiny.

"I think it's Scott Collins." Heather Cole, a field supervisor, changed the subject back.

"Scott who? What?" came from two people at once.

"'The Advocate'. I think it's him." Heather stated confidently.

Gerry Bennet, the only male on the staff, and the only African-American in the office at the moment, only grunted disagreement. He didn't mix in with the girls, not when they were all together like this anyway.

Nancy Carson, one of the two questioners, wanted more information. "Well, who is he?"

"He's a probation officer in Washington County. I heard that Warren Knoop was one of his cases. He probably was going to check on the perp and caught him in the act." Heather had everyone's attention now. Her theory had given rise to new speculation.

"After the act." Nobody heard Angel Akin's comment amid all the other excitement regarding the Advocate and all the possibilities.

CHAPTER 20

Father Tom Callahan had been treated and released from the "Center for Pedophile Priests" (that's not what they call it), but he still had his memories and he was still a monster. One of the things that made him different from all the other inmates, or participants at the Center, was that the, now defrocked, priest was also suspected of murder.

Sure, Callahan had pleaded guilty to 23 criminal sexual offences against little boys between eight and ten-(he was very particular) years-old, but he received no jail time, due to a deal that had been cut with a naive prosecutor by a highly paid lawyer retained by the Catholic church. The other, possibly more than a hundred, rapes of children he had committed had not been prosecuted because the short statute of limitations in Missouri had run out. Laws had a hard time keeping up with pedophiles.

The rape and murder of the little boy was also never prosecuted. There was no DNA evidence collected in those days. There was still no evidence against Father Callahan other than that both of the victim's brothers had told police, at the time of the murders, that their dead brother had said he was afraid of the priest. Father Callahan had been questioned, once, before he was quickly transferred to another parish. It came out later that the priest had raped both brothers when they were growing up, passing through that eight- to ten-year-old age group that the priest liked so much.

The victim had been found down by the Mississippi River, on the south side of St. Louis, only a few miles from the parish where then Father Callahan had practiced his faith and tended his flock. The archdiocese was very powerful in those days and the whole idea of a priest raping and killing little boys was not discussed or even considered. Those police detectives, and others who wanted to pursue the matter, found themselves suppressed, transferred or fired. The ex-priest still remained a suspect, but that was all.

Tom Callahan entered the church early, as he always did. He was comfortable here in Cape Girardeau, Missouri, where he was living out his retirement, with a full pension, in an apartment owned by the church. The bishop who had been helping him to continue his crimes all those years was facing his own accusations now, and was no longer a robe to hide behind, so Callahan kept a low profile these days. There would be a mass at 6:00 a.m; he never missed mass, and afterwards he would get ready for his monthly visit from his probation officer.

"Excuse me, Father Callahan, might I have a word with you?" Callahan was taken aback by the comment since no one called him "Father" any longer.

"Who are you?" He stopped his motion into the last pew to see who was speaking, then glanced around to see if anyone else was in the church; it was empty except for the two of them. It was then, when he looked away for a moment, that the ice pick slipped between his ribs. He hardly felt it.

"Oh, we're old friends." The whisper of breath was louder than the words in his ear. The former priest was frozen. He looked down and saw a hand up against his chest. Then the hand came away, pulling the thin piece of metal out of his heart. He realized that he had been stabbed with something, but when the hand pulled away everything sort of faded. They sat down together in the pew. Arm in arm. When the *ex*-child-raper/murderer/priest started to cool off, the rest of the shaft was pulled from the little wound it had made upon entering. There was no blood pressure now and there would be little or no blood.

Early mass goers found him sitting alone, sort of sleeping, there in the pew. Paramedics were called but it was presumed that the old man had died of a heart attack and no medical examination was performed.

The funeral home had been contacted to pick up the body from the church rectory where it had been carried. Everything was done to save the church and its members any undo stress or embarrassment.

He was remembered at the mass that day by worshipers who thought that an innocent old man had come to a peaceful end.

CHAPTER 21

Santucci was on his way back to southern Illinois. He was driving the "squad car" as Ariano had dubbed it. It was actually two Ford Crown Victoria police cruisers that they had welded together. The steel reinforced frame and oversized everything that Ariano had put on it was hardly noticeable. It was called the "squad car" because it had everything in it that was in a real highway cruiser-- lights, bells, whistles, and more. In fact every time he let Ariano have it for more than a few days, there was something new on it. This time it had a voice activated laptop and a G.P.S. locator built into the dash, under the twenty-five disk CD Player.

It had been a long hard day but he was happy to be leaving town instead of waiting for more flak to come down from above. That e-mail from the Advocate had started a firestorm in the media and at state police headquarters, too. The governor had called during Santucci's meeting with his superiors and simply

. stated that he wanted the whole matter cleared up immediately. The director of investigations, who made no bones about his dislike of Santucci, seemed happy to pass the governor's message on to the group before walking out to wait for Santucci's inevitable self-destruction.

When his phone rang, Milo's name and number popped up in his field of view, reflected on the inside of his windshield by a heads up display system. There was no handset and he had to say "Hello" three times before the computer recognized his voice and answered the call. Some of Ariano's stuff was a pain in the ass.

Milo's voice came out of sixteen speakers at once. "Diego, are you coming back down this way any time soon?"

"Is it Michael?" Santucci's foot pressed down on the accelerator without his realizing it.

"No, but we have located the parole officer and I thought you might want to talk with him."

He hated to drag things out of Milo. "Has he said anything yet that you think I might be interested in?"

"In a way. He has refused to say anything. He wants a lawyer."

"He wants a lawyer?" Santucci was hot. "I'll give him a....." He caught his favorite word before it got out. "...lawyer. What's his name again? Collins?"

"Scott Collins." Milo answered, and continued on, to give Santucci a moment to cool off. "He walked into the sheriff's office and said he didn't know anything about Warren Knoop and said that he wouldn't answer any questions unless he had an attorney present."

"Where's he at now?" Santucci had slowed down, both in his mind and on the ground.

"That's the other part. When I heard he was pulling a stunt, I sent Kozlowski out to pick him up and he wouldn't come to the door. Koz is sure he was in there. I've got a judge ready to sign a warrant if we can give him enough to back it up."

"What? I don't want to start issuing any warrants. The media will get a hold of it and we'll have them all over Collins. Then we'll never get anything out of him. Call him and invite him and his lawyer to a meeting. If they get stupid, we'll get tough."

That was fine with Milo; he liked it when Santucci got tough.

"Well, I'm halfway there now. Set the meeting up for later. I'll stop by your place first." He tried not to be obvious and failed.

"Michael is fine, Dago, but you might as well work out of here. It's centrally located and he's been asking for you. Polly won't let him call you and we're pretty boring as old people go."

Santucci was delighted that the little boy had asked for him, although he didn't say it. He also didn't admit how many times he had wanted to call and hadn't. For the next fifty miles, Santucci told Milo all about the supervisors' meeting and the governor's request, framed in the form of a demand.

CHAPTER 22

G ary Abbott wasn't the worst sex offender on the Illinois State Police Web site. He was the first. He was 45-years-old and was doing 60 months felony probation for two counts of predatory criminal sexual assault of a child. Gary's wife had been operating a day care center since 1997. Gary had been molesting the children left in her care since the beginning.

Sure, he had always been there to help with the children, for he was a perfect care-giver. He was always ready to change diapers or make sure that everyone went "potty" and got themselves wiped properly. And when Gary's wife would be out of the way for a while, Gary would lure one of the children into the bathroom and he would sexually abuse and molest them.

Finally, two of the victims told their parents, after who knows how many other children had been molested and been afraid to tell. To avoid prison time, a plea bargain was struck. Abbott pleaded guilty to an "act of sexual penetration of a victim who was unable to understand the nature of the act", a Class 1 Felony, two counts, 30 months probation for each.

The parents had agreed to the sentence mostly because they were afraid of the children being even more traumatized during a long criminal trial. Gary's lawyer had made it clear that he would pull no punches in defending his client. A win for him.

Gary was separated from his wife now. He lived in a motel that had been converted to apartments near Murphysboro, Illinois, just across the river from Cape Girardeau.

When there was a knock on his door, Abbott quickly blanked the pornography that he was addicted to from his computer screen. The probation department couldn't regulate his internet surfing. Once the screen was back to his aquarium wall paper, he hiked up his indignation and prepared to give anyone who would violate his privacy a hard time.

When Gary opened the door, he didn't have time to react. In one motion a hand reached in and grabbed him behind the neck and a hunting knife was rammed into his stomach, under his ribs, in an upward motion. The thrust of the knife, and the force of the attack, drove Gary back into his converted motel room, where he had just a moment to realize there was a knife in him before he coughed out a torrent of blood and sank to the floor. His visitor was gone when he looked up to see his last thing on earth.

CHAPTER 23

The death at the converted motel was only announced as a homicide and no names were released due to the fact that they couldn't find the next of kin to notify. Gary's wife wasn't bragging about their relationship and had moved out of the area. Also, the Jackson County sheriff's office couldn't figure out what kind of crime scene they had. The computer and CDs in the motel room were loaded with child pornography. More than enough to put the owner away for many years. But it appeared that someone had put the owner away already. It was probably some kind of weird jealous lover thing.

Santucci had a great evening. First of all, Michael had come running out of the house and jumped up and gave him a big hug. He seemed truly delighted to see Santucci.

"What happened to your car?" Michael asked after seeing Santucci get out of the black Ford.

"I switched to this one." Santucci thought that the Corvette might be sold. All he knew was that Ariano ran the business better than he ever had.

"I like the red one better." The boy didn't wait for a comment because he had bigger news.

"Diego, I was reading Harry Potter. The whole book." Michael looked up to Polly for confirmation and secrecy regarding how much help she had given him. She just smiled. That was good enough. He told Santucci all about how good he could read, and count, too.

"Good, that's great." He meant it. Santucci had heard of Harry Potter, but he didn't know who "The Count" was. He was genuinely pleased to see the boy and hear all about his day.

After going out for pizza and having a great time, Polly put Michael to bed with a little complaining by Michael and Santucci.   Santucci told himself that the kid needed sleep and settled his belongings into his room upstairs, next to Michael's. When he went downstairs he found Milo standing in front of the television. The point was that he wasn't sitting down in front of it. A computer generated voice came out of the speaker.

I AM THE ADVOCATE.   TODAY I TOOK ANOTHER MONSTER OUT OF THE WORLD. AFTER TODAY GARY ABBOTT WILL NEVER

HARM ANOTHER CHILD. ABBOTT PLEADED
GUILTY TO CRIMINAL SEXUAL PENETRATION
OF TWO CHILDREN. FOR THIS HORRENDOUS
CRIME HE WAS GIVEN PROBATION. HE WAS
INDICATED IN MORE SEX CRIMES BUT THE
COMPLAINTS FELL ON DEAF EARS AT THE
DEPARTMENT OF CHILDREN AND FAMILY
SERVICES. GARY ABBOTT WAS THE FIRST. IF
YOU ARE A MONSTER WHO HARMS CHILDREN,
BEWARE. I AM COMING FOR YOU. I URGE
ALL DECENT PEOPLE TO PROTECT OUR
CHILDREN.

Santucci was reminded of a line from a book
by Robert Ressler in which he quotes the famous
philosopher, Friedrich Nietzsche, "Whoever fights
monsters should see to it that in the process he does
not become a monster."

Milo looked over at Santucci. "I guess we're going
out."

Santucci tried to shake the thought and come
up with a realistic one. "I want to know where that
parole officer has been all day. And, by the way, do we
know who the hell Gary Abbott is?" Santucci reached
for his jacket while Milo was telling Polly that they
wouldn't be back for a while.

Santucci headed south in a hurry after they were
informed that Gary Abbott had been found lying in

the open doorway of his home, with a hunting knife stuck in him. They hit Route 13 off of the interstate and headed west.

"Do you remember what the message said?" Santucci asked Milo.

"Most of it." Milo mused over the message.

"That part about DCFS unfounding complaints. It seems that our subject has knowledge that is not public. He may be the parent of one of those children, or someone connected with DCFS somehow," Santucci speculated.

Milo voiced his similar concerns. "Why did he add that to the message? Trying to confuse us? It wasn't necessary, considering he had already confessed to murder and given sufficient reason to justify it to himself."

"Then there was the part about *another* monster, then something about *he was the first*." Santucci was puzzled by the conflicting statements.

"That's what the voice said. At the beginning it said *another monster* then, *he was the first*." Milo agreed.

"Abbott, the first." Santucci pondered, then the light went on.

"Milo, get on the sex offender web site and see if Abbott is on it, and if he is, see if he's the first one on the list."

Milo knew that the screen in the dashboard could access the internet but he was more comfortable with a laptop and opened Santucci's and got on line after a minute or two.

"You've got it. Here he is, number one, Gary Abbott, and the address is here too." Milo exclaimed. "I'm gonna have to think up a new brainy nick-name for you, Dago."

"Who's number two?" he asked.

Milo stopped smiling and looked back at the screen. "Javier Acevedo." Milo anticipated the next question this time. "And he only lives a few miles from here."

"Where?" Santucci was almost into Carbondale; luckily no traffic patrols were in place at the moment.

"Turn left at the next light."

They wound their way through the Shawnee National Forest, turning where Milo indicated. At the end of a long gravel lane they found several old trailers, the kind that the college-town slum landlords rented to desperate students for more than they were worth. Milo indicated the second one in the row. It was completely dark, the area lighted only by the headlights on the car.

Santucci put the spot light on the front door and they approached it from the sides. Milo had produced a pair of latex gloves and pushed on the door with a protected finger. It swung into the dark room. They couldn't see the entire room with the light from the car so they lit their little pocket flashlights before they entered cautiously.

The front room was in disarray, showing signs there had been a struggle. They found Javier Acevedo on the floor in the doorway of the bathroom where he had apparently tried to secure himself. There were several spots of what looked like blood on the back of his white T-shirt. He hadn't made it to the bathroom.

Milo knelt over the body, made some practiced moves, and looked up at Santucci. "At least four hours, Diego." Milo reported.

"Yeah, there are no lights on so it had to have happened before dark," Santucci observed in a more practical manner. He didn't notice Milo nod his head in agreement.

CHAPTER 24

There were still teams working on the crime scenes, although Milo and Santucci had gone home to get some sleep an hour or so after midnight. Before they left though, they reported in to headquarters and told them briefly that:

1. They didn't have any idea who the Advocate was. They didn't know if it was even one person, or a copycat.
2. They had sent out alerts and requests to make contact with and offer protection to the subjects who were next, alphabetically, on the sex offender list. (It was probably fortunate for them that the next six offenders on the list were from northern Illinois.)
3. There were no witnesses although they were still interviewing people.
4. They had collected evidence samples from the sites but they didn't look promising.

5. They agreed that it was most likely a male offender. The murder of Abbott had taken a lot of upper body strength and the subject had been held behind the neck in a military style maneuver. Acevedo had run away from his attacker, probably not something a man would do with a female attacker.

6. Both of them had been stabbed, but they weren't sure about the other weapon. It could be something like an ice pick, they thought.

7. They would await further developments, anticipating, while praying, that no more victims would surface.

8. The phone the killer used was purchased from Wal-Mart. Security video tapes had been requested from all the Wal-Marts in the area.

Santucci asked for FBI involvement, especially in the matter of tracking and monitoring the phone which the Advocate had used. He also asked for a bunch of court orders for monitoring and tracking. The killer had been wise enough to turn the phone off when he had finished using it. All they could tell at the moment was that the call had come from southern Illinois.

The FBI request was turned down by the director who refused to even ask anyone higher up. There was always animosity between agencies which Santucci could never understand.   Personally, he thought everyone should be on the same side. Years ago the FBI had picked up a kill order that had gone out for Santucci when he had been uncovered in the chop shop sting. They not only saved his life but also saved Santucci the torture that would have come first.

Santucci was willing to take help from any source, and to hell with the credit for accomplishments. One thing for sure, this Advocate was no longer committing justifiable acts, this was premeditated murder now.

Santucci rolled over about 8:00 a.m., apparently Michael had been prevented from checking Santucci's vital signs while he slept. He got up and went downstairs after getting ready for the day.

"Diego!" The little boy's smile could brighten any day.

"Good morning, Michael." He mussed the kid's shock of curly brown hair, genuinely happy to see the boy.

"Want some Cheerios? I love Cheerios." Michael held the box up with two hands.

"Me, too." Santucci started pouring the little rings into the bowl on the table.

"We've got bananas, too. Cheerios and bananas is my favorite." He wasn't kidding.

"Mine, too." Santucci agreed so quickly he surprised himself. Polly gave him a wry grin.

"Well, they are." Santucci defended himself to her.

That was the best way to have them. Santucci looked over at the little guy with his bright smile and couldn't help wondering why, or how, they had so much in common.

After eating, Michael was sent upstairs to take a shower. The kid loved the shower, and Santucci concentrated on his breakfast.

"Diego, can you take Michael to his counseling session in Marion? I have an appointment to attend a visitation with my CASA kids. I can pick him up afterwards so you can get back to work."

Although the homicides should have been first and foremost in Santucci's mind he didn't think twice about putting everything aside when Michael needed something, agreeing immediately.

"How many kids do you have, Pol? CASA kids, I mean." Santucci knew Polly's own children.

"On this case I have three, two boys and a little girl. It's a drug case. The task force busted a drug lab and the littlest one was on the floor playing with the empty cans from the chemical ingredients. The mother is almost dead from using meth. All of her teeth have fallen out and she only weighs 80 pounds. The father is looking at a mandatory ten-year sentence. It's a real shame." She looked off for a moment, visualizing more than she could say.

"Diego, what does 'k-s-t-l' mean?" Michael appeared in the doorway, with hair wet and blinking shoes. Santucci looked up from the bowl, where he was chasing the last few Cheerios around with his spoon; there were no banana slices left, they never lasted that long.

"K-s-t-l? I don't know what that means." Santucci tried to picture the word in his mind and drew a blank.

"That's what it says on the side of the truck," the boy added.

"What truck?"

"The one that's out in front." Just as the boy said that the doorbell started ringing. Santucci swallowed a curse, gave up on the last few floating rings and tossed the spoon down in disgust.

The reporter just started spouting the minute Santucci went to the door. The cameraman was shooting over her shoulder. Milo was still upstairs and Santucci felt that this intrusion was his fault anyway.

She got right to work. "Lt. Santucci, of the eighteen thousand sex offenders in the State of Illinois twelve thousand are not supervised. How are you going to protect them from the Advocate, alphabetically?" The dark-haired reporter was wearing a little red jacket and looked, to Santucci, as though she were from Southeast Asia. She held her microphone up for Santucci's expected answer. The only thing he noticed was that she was shorter than him, something he always noticed whenever he met a woman, regardless of the circumstances.

After he had the usual first thought out of the way, his second thought was an angry one. "Can't you people follow procedures? In a few minutes I'm going to come out of this building with a little boy. If you and your camera are still here, I'm going to impound that truck, have you all arrested for endangering a witness, and held until I'm contacted by the Missouri Attorney General personally. Won't that make a great story?"

He just looked at the reporter, the videographer, and the rest of the assembled technicians and dared them to do anything other than beat it. The camera sort of wilted. The reporter almost said another word, which would have been too bad for her, changed her mind and followed the rest of the crew towards their truck.

CHAPTER 25

M ichael didn't like the new car. Nobody waved, or even bothered to look at them while they were driving to the DCFS office. Michael was in the front seat in a new, and supposedly better, booster seat. Santucci was glad that Ariano had put a child-sensitive sensor in the air bag on that side.

"The red car was inappropriate," Santucci said, then asked himself what inappropriate meant and thought some different words were needed. "It was too small inside. I need more room for my work."

"Okay." Michael didn't argue, he just didn't like the car as much as the Corvette. Either did Santucci.

"Diego, we need to check on my mom. She's gonna need us to make sure she's all right."

"Okay." Santucci didn't argue. The kid was right, again.

After dropping the boy off and not accidentally bumping into Dr. Angel Akin, although he hung around for awhile, Santucci headed towards the office of the Illinois Department of Corrections, Parole Division, in Marion, to meet with Scott Collins, and his attorney.

Thinking about what the boy had said, Santucci made a phone call. Or rather he said "telephone" out loud five times before he heard a dial tone come out of his speakers, then he called out numbers until the car made the connection, on the second try.

When Jerry Feldman finally came on the line Santucci could tell that he wasn't in the mood for a conversation, especially not with old friends.

The first thing Santucci did was say, "Hello," and "how are you, Jerry?" Feldman took that as an opening for refusal of an imminent request.

"Diego, my hemorrhoids are hanging down to my knees, my calendar is backed up, I've missed three doctors appointments and my daughter just told me that she's in love with a guy who has a snake tattooed on his face. On his face, for Christ's sake."

"Use your own God for curses, Jerry."

"We're not even allowed to say his name, in vain or any other way." Santucci didn't have time for a lesson in Judaism.

"Jerry, I need you to find out what is going on with a woman named Glenda Fashe. She was arrested in Washington County. I want you to get her out of jail and into treatment for drug abuse."

"Can't you find women who are out of jail already to date?"

"I'm not kidding, Jerry."

"I know you're not. That's what's worrying me. You're a police lieutenant, you can't be bonding women out of jail. Who am I supposed to say my client is, if I'm asked?"

"What would you normally say if anyone asked, Jerry?" Santucci knew the rights fighter well enough.

"I'd tell 'em it's none of their..........damn business."

"That's why I'm calling you. Now will you do it?"

"Just between you and me, who are we doing this for?"

"For her son, who's four and three quarters." Santucci couldn't get over that quarter to five comment.

"Jeeesus."

Santucci started to say something and Feldman just said, "All right! Damn you!" and hung up.

CHAPTER 26

Santucci also called Milo and found out some things that might come in handy. Milo had the shoe imprint models. There was a small square heel that didn't match any of the shoes they had, but they did have one interesting match, A.J. Gilbert had been next to the bodies, on both sides, in fact. So he had lied.

Was there a chance that Sheriff A.J. Gilbert killed Warren Knoop and waited around the area for someone to discover the bodies and then pretended to happen by when a panic-stricken Noel Carlton ran into the street? Sure. But he didn't figure on the next two. He even had an alibi for the one of them. Santucci told Milo to stay with it and text message him while he was at the meeting.

The conference room was occupied when he was escorted there by the regional director, Mr. Drummond.

"Lieutenant, I can not believe that Scott Collins could have done anything wrong. Although, I also cannot understand why he has been so difficult to reach, and why he would only agree to this meeting if he could have an attorney present. Very puzzling. Of course we are going to attempt to have him dismissed if these things cannot be explained satisfactorily."

"Attempt?" You couldn't even fire people anymore. Santucci was only half listening to this guy.

Scott Collins was short and stout, but not fat. He's the right size, was Santucci's first thought. He was introduced to Collins and the lawyer, who was obvious. He was wearing a well-worn suit that had been nice once, little glasses on a chain around his neck and was holding a yellow pad in front of him. Drummond didn't wait around after the intros.

Before Santucci's butt even hit the chair the attorney pulled a little tape recorder out of his pocket and put in on the table between Collins and Santucci, then nodded at the lieutenant, as though that put Santucci in a certain position which assured his conduct.

"My first question........Scott, is why do you want to have this attorney here? You are a parole officer, a state employee."

"Mister Hartman is here at my request. To observe and......advise me."

Very cute, Santucci thought. "Where were you on the morning of Wednesday, April 6th?"

The lawyer spoke. "We are not prepared to answer that question at this time."

"I'll tell you what. Instead of me asking you questions, why don't you tell me what you are prepared to say....Scott." That pleased them. Santucci was counting to ten inside.

"I had nothing to do with the incident in Richview. I was assigned the Warren Knoop case but never worked on it and never had any knowledge of anything to do with Warren Knoop before his death. I have eyewitness alibis for both of the murders in Jackson County. That's all I have to say." He was very satisfied with himself. Put the cop in his place.

Santucci was so angry that he just sat there looking dumbfounded, praying for something to happen, not even caring what it was. If St. Michael came down and laid about with his sword, that would have suited him just fine. His cell phone started vibrating. It was on the table in front of him. He glanced at it, picked it up, looked at the display and smiled.

Santucci pointed at the lawyer. "You, out!" He pointed towards the door.

The lawyer was shocked; he looked down at the tape recorder to make sure it was still going around. Santucci picked it up and threw it at his head.

"I said out, get out!" Santucci started to jump over the table after the guy. The tape player had missed the guy's head by an inch, hit the concrete block wall and broke into a million pieces.

He backed away from Santucci's assault and fled the room. Scott Collins was frozen for a second but recovered nicely and started after his counselor.

Santucci grabbed Collins by the arm and spun him around slamming him into the wall behind the door. "I put up with this crap from you, Collins, you lying bastard, now I want you to know that you're the next candidate for a lethal injection."

Collins had started to protest until Santucci got to the part about the injection. Santucci reached over to the table and picked up his cell phone and showed it to Collins. He knew what the text message said. HOTLINE CALL TO DCFS CAME FROM COLLINS' PHONE.

Scott Collins slumped into a chair, all the fight gone out of him. "I didn't do it. I didn't do it," was all he would say, at first. He didn't say much worth hearing all told.

After a few minutes of this guy, Santucci couldn't figure out if he was telling the truth or not.

He told Santucci that he had found out that Knoop was living near a school and made the call to get DCFS to do his work. He continued to say that he wasn't in Richview at the time of the murders, but he wouldn't say where he was. He complained that he had more cases than anybody else. Overworked and underpaid, great excuse.

After Santucci had had enough of it he told Collins to get up; they were leaving. Santucci had decided to give the lawyer a break if he wasn't around when they came out of the conference room. He wasn't that smart. He was standing in the hallway talking menacingly on his cell phone and looking hard at Santucci.

Santucci picked up the cassette tape that had unwound all over the floor and had it in his hand when the lawyer started to make threats and demand the return of the tape.   Once in the hall Santucci looked toward the front door where Mr. Drummond stood nervously not wanting to witness anything. Behind him appeared the lanky form of Jim Kozlowski and the gentle giant Milo. It was always good to see those two.

"Before you say anything, counselor, I'd like to advise you that you, and your client, are under arrest. All rights and legal privileges apply, of course."

The lawyer shut up quick enough to show he was listening.

The attorney found his voice but Santucci waved him off and addressed Kozlowski.

"Jim, take these two over to the county jail and have them processed for obstructing a murder investigation and add conspiracy charges. Their statements are on the tape; combine that with the evidence of the phone call."

Kozlowski took the two, protesting all the way, and herded them back the way he had just come. Milo took the loose cassette tape and dropped it in an ever present envelope.

"What about the murder?" Milo asked, after the others had gone.

"I don't know, Milo. I figure he didn't do it, but we're going to have to find out where he was at the time. He refuses to disclose that. Although he's happy to tell you that he has an alibi for the last two murders. I don't know...tell you what we can do in the meantime. Who's the states attorney in this county?"

"The Italian guy, Calterra. You should get along well with this guy. He's got a reputation for being tough. His conviction rate is the highest in the state. Sex offenders get the maximum sentence. He doesn't even have opponents when he runs for re-election."

"Okay. Let's ask Calterra if he'll go along with charges on Collins. See if you can get him on the phone and I'll explain it to him. Then I want to have Marnie Marzulo call a press conference and announce an arrest in the Richview case. Then we parade Collins, in shackles, in front of the cameras and call him a person of interest, being held on lesser charges. Maybe, if there is a copycat on the second two, we might put him off any more killings if he thinks we have a suspect for Knoop. Just a shot, what do you think?"

"Sounds like a plan to me. What about the lawyer? You really don't want to arrest him, do you?" Milo didn't think it was a good idea.

"The parole officer deserves it. I was willing to cut him some slack if he had a reasonable excuse, but he tried to play me. As far as the lawyer is concerned, Calterra can cut him loose if he's learned his lesson."

"Lesson? What's the lesson?"

"If Calterra is a *real* Italian, he'll know what the lesson is." Santucci smiled at Milo. "Don't *ef* with Dagos."

"*Ef?*" Milo kidded Santucci.

"I'm trying to cut down on cursing; doctor says it makes my enzymes go up, or something."

Santucci filled him in on the interview and what he wanted regarding the press conference. He also told Milo to begin monitoring the home and cell phones of Scott Collins and to put a G.P.S. tracker on his car. Milo just nodded, all bets were off now.

CHAPTER 27

The next day Angel Akin was still not acting like herself. She wasn't proud of it, but she needed information if she was going to try to stop the nightmare she was living. And she had just gotten a lot of information. Although she had gotten it in a way that was out of character for her. It used to be out of character for her; now she was a liar and an eavesdropper.

"Lt. Santucci, I would be glad to meet with you," she had said to Santucci's request, adding, " Michael has been making progress which you'll want to know about.....and I guess you are looking for people who have access to our files." She anticipated his motive, she thought. She was going to have to keep a step or two ahead of this guy. That was why she mentioned Michael, she knew the lieutenant would agree to whatever she wanted if she dangled the child in front of him. Out of character.

When he arrived, at closing time, she had him wait in the front while she pretended to finish up some work. What she had done, however, when his phone rang, was sneak into the hallway and listen to Santucci's phone conversation with his boss. Santucci's half of it anyway, which was enough.

"Frank, I don't know if it will work."

"If he stops killing people, it will be worth it. And Collins is getting what he deserves."

"What about Acevedo?

"Yeah, he was a real peach. I hate to say that the guy deserved it but he was a bad actor. He did four years in the penitentiary for having sex with a 12-year-old neighbor girl, finished his probation and only had one more month to spend on the sex offenders list. He was going to celebrate by taking a trip to Thailand. A sex trip."

"That's what I'm saying. They have travel agencies that sell sex vacations. Although Acevedo was planning a special trip, sex with children."

"There were pictures and brochures in his trailer, and enough child porn on his computer to put him away for years."

"That's right. What's worse, you've heard about when people give money to an overseas children's charity, they sometimes send a picture back with a letter that's supposed to be from the kid?"

"Yeah. Well, that bastard, excuse my language, had letters, supposedly from children, written in a juvenile hand, on school notebook paper. They talk about how *big* they heard he was and what they want him to do to them when he comes to visit them. They are accompanied by digital printout photos of Thai children posed in seductive positions. It was disgusting really."

"No. Only the next six people on the sex offender Web site are covered. Nobody's going to get to them."

"Frank, there are 18,000 registered sex offenders in Illinois."

"Yeah, Frank, 18,000."

"I agree. But we can't guard them all."

"Well, the media is driving the story. Every sex offender in the state is being hounded, regardless of his number on the list. Especially those in the area. The television people are as likely to find the next body as anyone else. The pundits are analyzing every word of the statement the Advocate made."

"The voice? Did you ever check out your own groceries on a scanning machine?"

"That's the voice he used. You can buy the software anywhere. All he did was enter the statement in his computer and then play it back through the program that changed it to a computer generated voice."

"No, there's no way to trace it. We're setting up the bugs on the cell phone and when he uses it we'll be able to triangulate the signal."

"I want those subpoenas for the tracking and monitoring."

"No, I won't do anything until then."

"Wal-Mart is cooperating. They are sending all the video from the local stores. Maybe we'll get lucky and see the guy buying the phone on one of the tapes."

"It's all a long shot, Frank."

"No, I don't think it's the same person."

"The messages aren't the same."

"If I knew why, I'd be sleeping in my own bed tonight."

CHAPTER 28

"We'll take my car if you don't mind," Akin said, as she passed through the door he was holding for her.

"You didn't like my little red wagon?" Santucci kidded. She speared him with a blue eye as she turned the key in the lock.

"I'm driving the squad car today. Although Michael doesn't like it as much as the Corvette. Michael's going to be disappointed, too. I think Ariano sold the 'Vette." He gestured toward the black Ford parked near the door.

"How many cars do you have?" She followed him around to the passenger side.

"Between 10 and 15,000. Depending on how you count them. They're mostly in pieces."

"How many?" She waved the question away and he shut the door on her, going around to the driver's side.

"I never saw a squad car with an interior like this before." She rubbed her hand across the Cabretta leather seat which was also black. "How'd you get into this business again?"

"It's a long story." He wasn't telling.   And he wasn't sure what he was doing here or why he had agreed to go with her on this interview. Did she want a witness? Protection? Did she want to spend some time with him? Was he kidding himself? She sure smelled nice.

She told him about Michael as he followed her traffic directions. The boy was doing remarkably well. He was adjusting to the new situation. His mother now had an attorney, had been bailed out of jail and had signed herself into a secured rehabilitation institution. Akin couldn't figure out how that had happened. She said she was going to look into it. She thought it must have been some kind of grant program she hadn't known about.   Santucci didn't volunteer any of his own thoughts.

When they pulled into the parking lot of the Greater Christian Church, Santucci thought the little squat buildings didn't live up to the name. The preacher was happy to see them and escorted them to the room where they were going to interview Mr. Dixon. He explained how they supported their church members and how he had counseled Mr. Dixon and found him to be telling the truth and he couldn't understand why she had brought along a police officer.

"Lt. Santucci is studying our methods. He's not here in a police capacity. I'm just here to interview Mr. Dixon. You know there's been an 800 call and we have to follow up all calls." The preacher gave her a look that was dubious, but he remained hopeful.

Dixon wasn't there yet. They waited in a room that looked as though it doubled as a dining room. "Dr. Akin," Santucci emphasized the "Dr.," "how do you get stuck with going out and interviewing these people?" Santucci smiled to let her know he wasn't expecting a real answer. He didn't get one.

"It's a long story." She wasn't in a smiley mood. "I chose this place. It doesn't work if they're not in a place where they can feel comfortable." Santucci wanted to ask what 'it' was but there was a rap on the door followed by the preacher and Mr. Dixon. The preacher told them to call him if they needed anything and gave Dixon a firm pat on the shoulder before he left.

Jesse Dixon was fairly average. He was in his mid twenties, of medium size, had short brown hair, was clean shaven and was wearing a blue T-shirt with jeans. He acted confident and a little nervous at the same time.

"Jesse, I have to ask you about your girlfriend Jenny's daughter, Crystal."

"I want to know who called," was his answer to that statement.

"You know that we cannot divulge that information." She continued on without waiting for another question from him.

"You have been alone at the house with Crystal, haven't you?"

"If she doesn't have school, or something. I'm laid off at the moment."

"How old is she now?"

"She'll be 11 next week. We're planning a party." He smiled at the thought.

Angel Akin's voice droned on. Santucci sat back and tried to make himself invisible. Question and answer. The same questions different ways. Suggestions of scenarios that might have occurred at the house. Dixon deftly denied and seemed genuinely offended by the implied accusations. Back and forth. He stood his ground. Santucci was prepared to agree with the preacher. An hour went by.

"Maybe you were watching television and she was sitting on your lap and things just started to happen, and it just slipped in...." she said, again, in a different way.

All of a sudden, Dixon hesitated. Santucci was watching his eyes when they seemed to go out of focus. Dixon caught himself quickly and continued to deny any sexual activity with the child, but Santucci saw the change. Dixon was appalled, insulted, he was going to sue everybody. Another painstaking half-hour went by slowly.

"Maybe you were watching a tape and...." Santucci saw his eyes go out of focus again. One side of the brain retains and recalls memories, the other side conceives and constructs lies. The man was reliving an experience, one that had been powerful and couldn't be put out of his mind.

Akin spotted it too. She kept on with the same scenario, watching him closely. Then it was as though she had given him permission to speak.

He started slowly, his voice different, sobbing, finally pouring the whole thing out. He had been raping the child since that day, whenever he had her alone, but he didn't see it that way. He said he loved her. And she loved him.

"Excuse me, Mr. Dixon. Dr Akin, may I have a word with you?" Santucci couldn't take any more of this guy discussing having sex with the little girl as though it were something normal. And he couldn't understand how Akin just sat there and conversed with the fiend as though they were discussing the weather.

He took her across the hallway and through an exit door. They were in a little garden area surrounded by buildings. She followed him without comment. "Dr. Akin," he said formally, "We *are* going to arrest that guy, aren't we?" Santucci didn't know what to expect considering how she had acted toward the guy.

"Abso-fucking-lutely!"

Whoa. When she said it Santucci jumped back a little.

"Son-of-a-bitching-bastard! BASTARD! DAMN HIM!"

Santucci clearly understood how she felt now.

Her face was so red Santucci thought her hair would catch fire. She continued to curse, using every word that wasn't in the book. Santucci thought she was going to burst. Then she just stopped herself.

After a few moments of precious silence she said, "Diego, would you get a police car over here, please." Neither one of them realized that she had used his first name, as Michael did, casually.

"Have them take this piece of sh...crap to jail and hold him for predatory criminal sexual assault of a child." She accentuated each word as though it were a nail in a coffin.

Akin waited in the car while they took Dixon away. She wouldn't look at him again, not until she testified at his trial. A criminal investigation would be opened and evidence collected to support the charges. The child had already alluded to some things, which had prompted the 800 call, hopefully she would be able to tell more.

Dixon was led away in cuffs, sobbing, a broken man. Not broken enough, Santucci thought. The preacher assured Dixon that they would get him an attorney and have him released. Santucci had an argument with himself. Did a person like this deserve to have an attorney? Did he deserve to have a chance to do this to another child? Santucci lost both arguments.

CHAPTER 29

"I have to admit, I'm learning a lot." Santucci tried to break the ice with a lame comment. They came easy when he was with her. "I mean, not something that I really wanted to know." He was driving east on Route 13, going nowhere.

He made a little admission. The interview had really shocked him. "I couldn't believe how he just talked about it so casually. I hope the child is all right." He said seriously.

"She's been sexualized now." She hated the truth sometimes.

"Sexualized?" He was always asking for more, good or bad.

"Did you ever hear the expression, you can't 'un-ring' a bell? The child knows what sex is now. And she doesn't think it's something special that two people, who are in love, want to share. She thinks it's something entirely different, and she'll be lucky if she can adjust and have a normal life."

"I guess it's all about sex." He involuntarily supplied another lame comment.

Her mind had been on something else, but she spoke up. "It's not all about sex." You need to learn a few things Lieutenant, she thought.

He looked over at her. She took that as a request to continue. "It's not about sex; it's all about power and control. Sure, sex is one of the things that people use to assert their control over a child but that's just one of the ways people abuse children."

"We had a case where a child presented at school with suspicious burns. When we investigated it we found that the mother was torturing the child and her boyfriend was a willing helper. The little boy was beaten, burned with cigarettes. It went on for years. There was a lot of mental abuse also. She hated the child, mostly because he was the image of his father, a vicious man who abused the woman and finally drank himself to death."

She paused for a breath, remembering the story too well. "When I went to the house, it was like a pig sty. All except the boy's room. It was spotless. He kept it that way to minimize the excuses for them to torture him. There was a hasp for a padlock on the outside of the door and the light was controlled from the hallway. No window in the room. He's in a good home now, but he still keeps his room spotless. Those are the worst, where the mother, the nurturer, is the assailant. The child might recover well if hurt by a stranger, but when the child is betrayed by the parent.......well that is difficult to overcome." She was quiet for a few moments. "I'm sorry I got so upset before. You'd think I'd be used to it." She apologized.

Santucci just drove, afraid to comment.

"You wanted to know why someone with a Ph.D. in psychology gets stuck interviewing these monsters?"

He clearly wanted to know, but wasn't going to say it.

"People tell me things." He took his eyes from the road for a glance at her. She was looking down at her hands which were wringing themselves.

Santucci made a little *'umm'* sound, hoping it would signal to her that he was willing to listen.

"I don't know what it is. Ever since I started working for DCFS, they confess to me when they won't even talk to anyone else. I don't know how it happens. I just keep on plugging away and sooner or later they cave and tell me everything. It's something with the eyes. I can tell when they're going to crack."

Santucci definitely agreed with her. He didn't know how she did it either. He also needed a break from this stuff. "Well, I could go for a steak and a glass of wine." Santucci looked over and showed his most charming smile. "How about you?"

She smiled back and took too long to answer. "Okay. Turn here."

The restaurant she took him to was just off the highway. Chuck's Place was half bar and half restaurant, with two worried waitresses working a packed house. Since Akin was obviously known in the place they got the next table. Santucci relaxed and was delighted to find a Cabernet, that he thought was extinct, on the wine list for a ridiculously low price.

"I'll have the filet mignon and make it rare." Knowing how they liked their steaks cooked in southern Illinois he added, "Make that extra rare. And underline it." Akin smiled at him, it was beautiful.

"I'll have the catfish, Donna." Everybody called her Angie.

"I'm sorry." Santucci was suddenly upset. "I ordered red wine without asking what you were going to have for your entree."

He looked up for the waitress who was working on another order already. Akin smiled, thinking how out of place *Mister Food Etiquette* would sound ordering white wine for her, because she was having fish, in this joint.

"Diego," she did it again. "Do you eat a lot of catfish?"

He admitted he didn't. He preferred raw fish but there wasn't a sushi bar or a Japanese within a hundred miles of them.

"Catfish is more like meat than fish. Red wine doesn't hurt it any." There was the smile again. He liked it.

When the food came she ordered a beer and looked at him cattily "We've got time for a long story now."

He remembered the question. "How did I get in the car business?" He smiled at the thought. He always did.

"You have to go back a ways. Did you ever see a Saturday Night Live skit back in the 80s where the characters played sports fans in Chicago?"

She thought about it for a second and smiled, but she wasn't going to do the shtick.

"Right, you remember." He said. "The parts they played, saying things like, 'Da Bulls, Da Bears?'" She nodded, smiling widely.

"Well I'm from, 'Da Neighborhood.' "

"What?" She was laughing out loud.

"Do you want to hear the story or not?"

"All right. I'll stop laughing."

"Just smile." He continued, "When they portrayed the characters with their heavy Chicago accents, I'll bet the people in my old neighborhood didn't get the joke. Where I was raised, everyone speaks with a heavy accent. Dees, Dem. One, two, tree. Like that."

She had quit laughing, but was smiling beautifully.

He went on, "When I graduated from Catholic high school,"

Her eye brows went up.

"I enrolled at SIU."

Another eyebrow move.

"That was back in the days of Viet Nam."

No reaction, at least she seemed to know what Viet Nam was.

"So, for my first semester I did the *Animal House* thing, flunked every course and was drafted into the Marines one month later."

"Marines?" she asked.

He answered the next question before she could ask it. "People don't remember it really, but back then the Army and Marines both drafted personnel."

"So after I got out," skipping two years, "the state police were looking for recruits and I passed the test which I think at that time was 'touch your finger to your nose.'"

"Then I got picked out of rookie school and placed in a deep cover situation." He was looking off, thinking, now. "The FBI chose me partly because I was from a place in Chicago where organized crime has always existed. They got me a 'bona fides' from the Chicago 'Family' and installed me in a chop shop in East Saint Louis. That went on for about five years, and in that time, I did a lot of business. Both illegal and legal. Computers were the coming thing, and Ariano and I set up international sales on line."

He thought he better explain his cousin. "Ariano is my cousin, on my mother's side. If you think Italian families are tight, you won't believe the Mexicans. He worked for me from the beginning. I had it cleared with the Feds, but Ariano didn't care whether we were legal or not. All he worries about is sending money to Mexico. We probably own a couple of towns down there by now."

She smiled brighter at that.

"So the Feds busted hot car and chop shop operations all over the world. Then the operation was shut down," another skip of a bad memory, "the government held an auction and I bought the whole thing. We knew where everything was and how to make money legally. Ariano likes the business and I get to drive a different car every week. And that's how I have 10,000 cars." He gestured with his hands as though he were a magician.

CHAPTER 30

When they were almost finished eating she whispered conspiratorially; she was starting to feel better. "So you were in the Mafia?"

He smiled at her and told her the truth, thinking about why people tell her things. "There's more Mafia on television than in real life." He paused for a second. "In real life you have the sheep and the wolves."

"Sheep and wolves?" She was leaning across the table.

"Most of the people in the world go about their lives and conduct themselves with relative civility. Crime is abhorrent to the sheep. Then there are the wolves. They are professional criminals who prey upon the sheep for money, power, or just for the fun of it." He was talking too much. The Cabernet was 14.5 percent alcohol, he reminded himself.

She was enjoying herself though. She brought out that conspiratorial smile. "So what are you Santucci? Wolf or sheep?"

He smiled back, having set her up for this. "Why, I'm the sheep dog, Angel." Then he thought he'd better change the subject, before she asked for more details about his past.

"And what do you want to be when you grow up?"

She changed the smile menacingly when he asked her.

Santucci hurried on. "You don't want to be out here interviewing these fiends all your life. Nobody could stand that for too long." He sounded concerned all of a sudden.

Akin thought about it for more than a second then seemed resigned to telling him something about herself that she didn't share with others. "I'd like to have my own children's advocacy center."

He could tell that she had given it some thought as she went on with her dream. "It would have all the latest technology. Hidden cameras and two-way mirrors. Comfortable play rooms designed for children. Good therapists, who can be fired if they don't do their job or keep up with the latest studies in their fields. In short, I'd like to have a center where the children came first. Where we didn't have to worry about budget cuts or politicians mandating things that don't work."

Santucci sat back and listened, enjoying this as much as he had anything in recent memory.

She was rolling now. "I'd have a day care center where the parents could monitor their children online. Oh, there's a lot more but...." She stopped abruptly, looking down.

Santucci noticed that she had glanced over his shoulder before she stopped talking. She just sat there for a minute and then looked at him and faked a smile. Then she looked up and Santucci felt a presence coming up behind him. He didn't move. Her face was animated enough to warn him if he had to duck.

"Hi, Angie, what brings you back to old Chuck's?" The man who had come to their table was about 5'10", well built, with thick hair and cowboy-looking clothes. The silver belt buckle he was wearing on his jeans was as big as a saucer. He didn't bother to look at Santucci, waiting for Angel Akin to answer his question.

She spoke to Santucci. "This is Kyle. He's my ex-husband. The last time I saw him I was wearing a cast on my arm. One of a series he gave me over the years."

Santucci stiffened.

Akin finally addressed her ex. "Kyle, what I do is none of your affair. Just because Susan speaks to you doesn't mean that you don't owe me fifteen thousand and change in back child support for the last ten years."

It was obvious that Kyle had been drinking before he got to Chuck's Place.

"You can forget that honey. You ain't never gonna see a dime of that. Didn't I teach you anything about me? Or should I say, didn't you learn anything during the last ten years you've been on your own?"

He snorted a laugh, turned and went over to where he had a friend at the bar. Santucci had everybody in the place pegged now. Now that he wasn't relaxed any longer. Santucci motioned for the waitress who had been hovering.

"Would you like another beer?" he asked Akin, as though Kyle had never appeared.

"Uh. No?" She answered and smiled up at the waitress.

"Bring me a bottle of Samuel Addams," he told the girl, and added, "don't take the cap off." She gave him a queer look but went to do as she was asked.

"I'm sorry about that," she said when they were alone.

"Sorry?" He reached across the table taking her hand.

When she didn't pull it away, he hurried on, "There's nothing to be sorry about. He's had a little to drink is all. Not a problem." He would have gone on but she pulled her hand away and looked at him seriously.

"When you grow up in a rural community, you either go away and seek a career or get married and have a family." She wanted to talk so he listened without comment.

"We were married young. We had a baby. A little girl, Susan. She's in college now. On a full academic scholarship," she added with pride. "Kyle was a coal miner. He worked hard and made good money. We did very well at first. Then the EPA decided that southern Illinois coal was too high in sulfur and the mines started to close. Kyle lost his job."

Santucci's beer came with an opener that they gave you when you bought paint at the hardware store.

"He wanted me to work. And I did. But I also wanted to go to school. He didn't like that because he didn't want me to do better, or be more educated, than he was. He wanted me to work at McDonalds. No kidding." She smiled at Santucci's raised eyebrow.

"He was going to do this, and that. Got us into debt with different ideas for businesses. He liked to hunt, so he tried things in that line. They all failed. Then he started drinking heavily and started in on me." She looked away remembering bad times.

"When I got my Associates Degree from John A. Logan College, he broke my arm and blacked both of my eyes. That was the day before graduation. Obviously, I didn't make the ceremony. It took me five years to finally get away from him. My daughter doesn't remember much of it. I shielded her the best I could, although you can't hide broken bones. So, now she's grown up, loves her father, and I don't dwell on what he used to do to me."

"I'd like to go home now, if you don't mind."

Santucci sat up quickly, ready to carry her out of the place as though it were on fire, if necessary. The waitress came with the check, which he couldn't believe was so low. He threw some money on the table, probably matching her tips for the entire week, and went to hold the chair for Akin. She shook her head and helped herself up.

Her ex-husband had positioned himself near the door where he was drinking with the friend he had come in with. Santucci tried to place himself between Dr. Akin and the bar as they left. Kyle stepped away from the bar as they passed, reached behind Santucci and grabbed Akin by the elbow.

"And I want you to know I ain't..." That was all Santucci heard him say before Kyle started screaming.

Angel Akin had him by the fingers which she was bending in a direction that they weren't designed to go. Kyle's arm, the one he had used to touch her with, was extended. Akin bent those fingers until they were breaking. Then she kicked him in the stomach. He would have fallen, but the leverage she was exerting on his arm and shoulder kept him on his toes.

The friend who was with Kyle started for Angel Akin. He reached out and his shoulder and arm exploded with pain when Santucci smacked him on the clavicle with the unopened bottle of Samuel Addams beer. The guy turned, his right arm hanging uselessly, and Santucci gave him the "no-no" finger. He decided to stay on the sidelines and nurse his arm.

Santucci looked back to where Akin was lecturing Kyle where he was writhing on the floor. "....and don't you ever come near me again. Don't you ever talk to me again. You piece of shit..."

Santucci took a chance and touched her on the arm. She whirled and caught herself before she started in on the next victim. "This is where we run out and jump on our horses and make a get-a-way before the sheriff arrives." He escorted her to the door, watching his back.

CHAPTER 31

"Susan?" Angel Akin was on her cell phone. Santucci and she had run to the car, laughing like children fleeing from the scene of a broken window. They were heading back to her office now, where her car was parked.

"I wanted you to know that I just ran into your father."

"I've just been talking with him, Mom. He's on the other line," her daughter related. Susan was away at school, in Champaign-Urbana.

"Good. Tell him that I meant what I said. He's put his hands on me for the last time."

"Couldn't you get an order of protection, or whatever, to make him stay away from you?" Susan wanted to settle the matter peaceably.

"If he doesn't leave me alone, he's going to need an OP for me." She'd had her fill of letting others protect her inadequately. Kyle had violated court orders on several occasions.

"So I've heard. Mother, he says you kicked him and broke his fingers," she scolded.

"I didn't hurt him that badly." Akin couldn't hide the exhilaration in her voice.

"He says he can't breathe." The daughter was concerned; she had family problems.

"When you can't breathe, you can't talk either. Tell him to go see a doctor. He's still drinking and, oh yeah, tell him that he still needs anger management counseling. I've heard that he's been pounding on that girl he's living with now."

Susan was quiet on the other end. She knew more about the things her father had done than her mother realized, but he was her father.

Finally Susan spoke, "I can't leave him hanging on...."

"Fine. Honey, tell him whatever you like. He's your father and you love him. If you ask my opinion, that's the only thing he's got going for himself. I love you Honey, bye."

"Bye, Mom. I love you too." They disconnected.

She looked over at Santucci. "Do you still have that beer?"

"Kyle's friend was asking for it, so I gave it to him." Santucci gave her a conspiratorial look.

They laughed together. Santucci seemed about to ask her something when his phone rang. "Milo," he said.

She listened.

"Well, is either of them our guy?" He listened for a few moments.

"Maybe our luck will change. I wish we could get the Feds on this but they won't go for it."

"Yeah, try looking for anything that we can use to get them on with us. I could really use the resources that I know they have. It would be nice if we could pin one of these out-of-state cases on our guy."

"Okay. I'll see you then." He put his phone down.

"Did they catch the guy?" Akin asked casually but listening for the answer intently.

"They caught two of them." He didn't make her ask him to explain.

"A guy in Oregon stabbed a man who had raped his daughter. Stabbed him about forty times. They caught him walking down the street, covered in blood. He told the police he was the Advocate."

"Oh." She tried to hide her dismay.

"And the other one?" She hoped she didn't sound too inquisitive.

"Another guy called 911 claiming to be the Advocate and said he had killed two sex offenders and was going to kill all the sex offenders in California. They went right out to the address that he had called from and found him sitting on the sofa making more threatening calls. They're checking on the 65,000 sex offenders registered in California to see if any of them have recently become dead."

"Sixty five thousand registered. Even though that sounds staggering, the figures go up every year, in every county, in every state." She knew the statistics all too well.

"I have to tell you this is overwhelming to me. I'm a police officer, yet I never realized how many people prey on children." He didn't mind making the admission.

"Everybody wants to do something about it, but the fact that children don't vote remains a factor in their lives. People say, "Our children are our future", but to the legislature they're just an expense item. Do you know the story of Mary Ellen?" She looked over to Santucci who shook his head, more things he didn't know.

"Up until the 1870's children had no rights; not that they have many now, but they were chattel in the past. They were not recognized as persons. There was a child named Mary Ellen. Her parents were dead and she was given, by the authorities, to a couple named Connolly. She was severely abused and neglected. It became so bad that a neighbor tried to get the police to do something and found that there were no laws against abusing children. Finally the neighbor appealed to the founder of the SPCA. There were laws against abusing animals, but not children. He took up her case and had it tried under animal abuse laws. The child was taken away from those people. The case caused such a public stir that within a year there were organizations forming that began to defend children." She could tell that Santucci was a little stunned.

She changed the subject quietly. "I heard that Noel Carlton was released."

Santucci's mind was on something else. For a moment, she thought he hadn't heard her. And she couldn't say it again. Then he answered. "Yes, they let him go. We were only keeping him so the media wouldn't hound the poor guy to death. Once we named Scott Collins as a person of interest we were able to let Carlton go without any fanfare. I felt sorry for the guy. When you asked about him on that first day, I knew he wasn't going to be charged but I couldn't tell you. Sorry I had to do that." She could feel him looking at her. She had to say something.

"Oh, that's all right, I understand." She couldn't help but add, "I'm sorry, too."

He didn't comment. They drove on in silence.

They arrived back at the DCFS offices. "Well, Lieutenant, you certainly know how to show a girl a good time." She faked a smile.

"Maybe we can do it again. You can show me some more about how that anger management stuff works." He smiled back at her. She got it, but wasn't smiling any longer.

"I guess you're with my daughter on that. Maybe I should have controlled my anger a little more tonight."

When she looked too thoughtful, Santucci continued quickly, before he lost his chance.

"I'm not with anyone on anything." He didn't want to blow his chance. "I was just wondering if we might go out sometime?"

"What? Oh, sorry."

"Sorry?" He blew it.

"No, not that. We can go out again." She didn't sound as though she meant it, but then she added, "Next weekend I'll be in Chicago for a conference, but maybe the week after that....."

She got out of the car; it was an awkward moment. He waited until she was in her car and moving before he headed off.

CHAPTER 32

During the week the Advocate had five more copycat crimes, two in New York, one each in Ohio, Arizona, and Florida. Attorneys for sexual predators were on every television station demanding civil rights, by way of protection from the public, for their clients. There were doctors, social scientists and law enforcement experts discussing every aspect of the crimes. The media was having a field day.

Thursday morning, Brenda Bluford was on her way to the grocery store to make the butcher cut her some ribeye steaks, two inches thick. Her boys wouldn't eat the skinny ones that everybody else purchased from the meat case. She demanded, and got, her way. And then all she would do was slide her Link Card through the reader to pay for it all. That was the best part.

The court had managed to take two of her daughters away from her but she still managed to qualify for aid. Brenda had made a career of welfare; she knew how to work the system. She would get her daughters back too, she promised herself, then she would take care of those little tattletales. Talked up a blue streak to those bastards at DCFS, they did. What was the big deal anyway? "It's just screw'n," she had told the investigators defiantly.

Distracted with thinking about everything she was going to do to everybody, while she was getting her huge bulk situated, she suddenly realized there was someone standing at the car door when she reached to close it. She looked up. Because the rising sun was behind the person, all she could see was a silhouette.

"What the f..?." She never finished the question. The Advocate pressed a button on a baton and a metal spike shot into her eye, penetrating her brain. Her head lolled over. The six-inch spike was pulled out, and her car door was finally closed with Brenda Bluford slumped against the wheel. Since her boys didn't work and slept most of the daylight hours Brenda wasn't found until the mail carrier went down the block.

The call came into the 911 dispatcher in the little town in Union County. The monitors were on it immediately, calling in the units who were standing by and sending them all towards the area where the call was coming from. It turned out that the caller had probably been sitting on the side of the interstate in a rest stop.

CHAPTER 33

"I AM THE ADVOCATE: UNDER THE 'B'S' WE HAVE A MONSTER NAMED BRENDA BLUFORD. HERS WAS THE WORST CRIME--- BETRAYAL BY THE NURTURER. SHE WILL NOT BE AROUND TO VIOLATE HER CHILDREN ANY LONGER. THIS MOTHER OF SIX ALLOWED HER BOYFRIEND, AND MALE MEMBERS OF HER FAMILY, TO HAVE INTERCOURSE WITH HER OWN DAUGHTERS. WHEN SHE WAS ACCUSED, SHE TRIED TO COVER UP HER ATROCITY BY FORCING THE GIRLS TO HAVE SEX WITH A NEIGHBOR, THEN THREATENED THE GIRLS WITH DEATH IF THEY TOLD AUTHORITIES.   WOMEN CAN BE SEX OFFENDERS, TOO. THEY SHOULD BE KILLED IF THEY HARM A CHILD. I URGE ALL DECENT PEOPLE TO PROTECT OUR CHILDREN.

Santucci was listening to the computerized voice on his satellite radio when his phone rang. He'd found out how to turn off the voice activation and pressed a button easily.

"I heard it, Milo. I'm on the way. Tell me what you know."

"The guy made the call just after the body was found and the Union County Sheriff sent a car out. Seems he may be monitoring the radio signals.

"He also has information about his victims that only people with access can have."

Santucci was speeding down the interstate with little strobe lights flashing front and rear. "This can't be a disgruntled parent any longer."

"We checked out every relative of every victim six ways to Sunday already. Somebody has to have seen the guy. It wasn't that early in the morning." Milo was frustrated.

"Wish in one hand..." Santucci let the thought trail off. "So tell me something good."

"The media made such a big stink about Acevedo's sex with children vacation to Southeast Asia, that the Feds made a bunch of arrests and the UN is appointing a special Czar to look into it. There's a Czar for everything now days," Milo added with distaste.

"What's good about that? Well, I guess it's good but I need something here."

"There've been eight copycat murders," Milo said casually.

"You're making my day. I thought it was five." All Santucci had heard was what was on every form of communication used by man.

"We're letting the public think it's five. Two are still under investigation and they don't want to release any information. And I was saving the last one for you." Milo was the best and he had an irritating sense of humor; you had to put up with it.

"Milo! Come on, man." Santucci hated to drag stuff out of people. Then he had another thought. "How do you know about copycats that no one else knows about?" A second later he said, "Forget it, just tell me please.......wait.....Milo, I've got an incoming, I'll call you back."

"Diego! I'm going to school tomorrow!" Michael voice screamed out of sixteen speakers gleefully.

"You are?" Santucci was suddenly grinning from ear to ear.

"I get to go on the bus! It's preschool." Which was obviously better than regular school.

"How did all this happen so fast?" Santucci wondered.

"Doctor Angel called Polly and told her I should go." The boy was beaming.

"Doctor Angel called and said you could go to school?"

"It's probably because she knows I can read.......... and count!" Don't forget how important the counting is.

"Does she call often?" Santucci queried cautiously.

"Oh yeah, we talk all the time. I really like her."

Possibly thinking about conversations with Doctor Akin, the boy changed the subject. "Diego, do you know how my mom is?"

Santucci had to think about his answer for a moment, "I know she is in a place where they will help her with the smoking and stuff, but....." Santucci looked at the caller ID on his dash display. Strangely enough the answer to the boy's question was on the other line. "......Michael, I've got another call. It's the man who will know what's going on with your mom."

"Okay, Diego. Call me back when you have a chance," the boy said, as though ending a business call.

Shaking his head and smiling, Santucci pushed a button on the steering wheel. "Jerry, how we doin'?"

"Diego, I have the official and the unofficial."

Santucci sighed, "Just lay it all on me, Jer."

"Court is tomorrow. We can get the charges dropped. The sheriff down here is an idiot. He screwed up the paper work so badly I could get her off the murder rap, if she did it."

Santucci let that thought roll around in his mind for a second. "So what's the unofficial?" he prompted finally.

"If she stays in the institution and completes recovery they'll lay off of her, but she's definitely being terminated on the little boy." Jerry knew Santucci wasn't going to like that; he didn't like it either.

"Isn't there an appeal or something?"

"Just a waste of time and money. Believe me, Diego. She was ordered by the court to walk the kid to school. And the kid wasn't just killed, she was.... damn....her picture's been on TV about a million times already. The boy is going to be adopted out. Bet on it."

"Adopted." It sounded like the worst word in the world to Santucci.

CHAPTER 34

Paul Barton was a teacher and counselor at the prestigious Chesswood Adacemy. That is until the FBI raided his home and confiscated thousands of CDs and tapes picturing children being sexually abused in every manner imaginable. Mister Barton, as he was known to the school boys he taught, counseled, and molested, was also pictured as a star performer in many of the scenes. His victims were runaways, local boys and the children of the wealthy who trusted him with their greatest possessions.

Mister Barton was out on bail, though. It was high, but the child pornography business paid heavily and he had been in the business for years. Sure, the Feds had a few things on him. His multiple post office box scheme was easily unraveled by them and his worldwide enterprise was now exposed along with all of his contacts. But they had raided his house with a warrant that had the wrong address on it. His lawyer was sure that they could get all the incriminating CDs and tapes, especially the ones that Mister Barton had starred in, thrown out of court.

Things were looking up until Paul Barton came home and found someone waiting behind his door. He almost found him waiting behind the door. Mister Barton was dead before he realized anything really. The door had been no problem; the Advocate was getting good at this.

■ ■ ■

"So Milo, tell me what you've been saving for me." Santucci still hadn't made it to Union County. Illinois was a big state, he was constantly reminded.

"There was an ex-priest who had a heart attack over in Missouri."

"And?"

"Well, when the undertaker pumped some embalming fluid into him he sprung a leak. Looks like someone stuck an ice pick in the old guy," Milo was loving this, "and he was a pedophile, over 200 perps."

"We'll have to do 'em all," Santucci was thinking out loud. He didn't have to tell Milo how happy he was with this development.

"The Feds are already working on it. They called Springfield and informed them that they were on the case. There's no asking now."

The light went on in Santucci's head. "That's how you know about the other copycats. You've had the Feds in all the time."

Milo agreed reluctantly. "Us lower echelon personnel like to keep each other informed. Nothing formal. You know."

"Yeah, I know. Too well. What about the priest? Why didn't the killer brag about him?" Santucci asked.

"Good question. The priest was before Abbott, and he said Abbott was the first."

Santucci rolled that one around for a moment then switched the gear a notch. "Do you think there's a second victim this time too? He didn't mention Acevedo in his first message. Maybe he's got another one waiting to pop up." It was just a thought, a bad one.

"I hope not," was the only thing Milo could say. Hopes were dashed a little while later when Mister Barton was found dead in his front hall.

CHAPTER 35

Angel Akin didn't want to accompany Bonnie Wheatherlow to the court hearing for Glenda Fashe, but she didn't want her to go alone. When she pulled up at the court house she saw a familiar vehicle, Santucci's squad car.

Inside the courthouse, Santucci was looking around in a confused state. There were people everywhere, going from one clerk's office to another. The second floor, the center of which was open and could be viewed from the lobby of the first floor, was packed with people going to or from one of the courtrooms that lined the entire second story.

He had passed the security checkpoint, not identifying himself as a police officer. He didn't carry a gun and had left his phone in the car since they were being allowed in fewer and fewer places every day. That was fine with him. Santucci saw Sheriff A.J. Gilbert speaking to a little woman flanked by a cameraman and went the other way. At least only the local stations were covering this aspect of the case.

"Hello, Lieutenant." Santucci turned to see a face that he recognized, then took a long second to remember who it was.

"Jack Crocker." The man said, extending his hand.

Santucci remembered him. "Right. How've you been?" Santucci took the extended hand for a regular shake.

"Been busy. Just dropped off a couple of INS cases, illegal aliens."

"Mexicans?" Santucci was partial to Mexicans, even alien ones.

"No. There's not a lot of Latinos around here. These three were Polish. They come through Chicago and spread out down here. I catch 'em and ship 'em back. Irish too, a lot of them." "How are you doin?" Crocker asked. "Catch your Advocate?"

"No."

"You lookin' for the court room where the Fasche girl is?" Crocker asked.

"Yeah, I was." Santucci answered a little uneasily.

Crocker pointed up to the second floor. "On the corner, room # 8. I saw it on the docket and thought I might catch Dr. Akin or Bonnie Weatherlow, the case worker on my case. I wanted to thank them for setting up my visitations and everything."

"How's your little girl?" Santucci asked, more interested in the child's welfare than he realized.

"She's doing fine. Real well. I see her every week, for two hours at a time now." He sounded very pleased.

"Well, I better get up there." Santucci gestured up towards the courtroom. They shook hands again and Santucci headed for the marble staircase in the corner of the lobby.

* * *

When Dr. Akin walked into the courtroom she saw Lt. Santucci standing up in front speaking with a man in a suit. She remembered who the man was a second later. He was Glenda Fashe's attorney, Mr........ Feldman. They finished speaking momentarily and Lt. Santucci took a seat in the first row of benches. She had something to tell him and now was as good a time as ever. She walked up the aisle and stopped next to him.

"Hello, Lieutenant."

He looked up when she spoke. Dark wavy hair with silver temples. Naturally tanned and Roman looking, he was wearing a tiny pair of gold rimmed reading glasses. He casually folded the glasses and put them in his jacket pocket. In the same motion he put the papers he had been reading down on the side away from her.

He gestured to the pew-like bench next to him. "Hello, Doctor, pull up a bench?"

"What are you doing here?" She got the question in first, but it didn't help. He asked one in return.

"I could ask the same question of you." Did he sound defensive?

"Sheriff A.J. Gilbert and the state's attorney want to make their re-election promises good so they subpoenaed half of my office. I don't think they have a case," she finished.

"That's what I've heard," he said.

She looked over at him, maybe expecting him to answer her question, but he was watching them bring Glenda Fashe into court. She was thin and gaunt and let her attorney do all the talking.

After the case was over, and all the stipulations had been stipulated to, they led Glenda Fashe out of the court room. Santucci hadn't commented during the entire proceedings. They got up and left the courtroom together. Akin felt that Santucci had wanted to speak with Mr. Feldman again, and she had ruined it. He could talk to him later, if he wanted. She wasn't sure she would have the courage to say what she had to say, later.

"Did you see Jack Crocker?" he asked her in the hall, giving her another moment to avoid telling him.

"No, was he here?"

"He said he was looking for you or Miss Weatherlow to say thanks for setting up the visitations with his little girl. I heard she's doing well," he added.

"She's not doing all that well." Akin sighed, there was more to an attack on a child than just the initial incident.

"She's not?" Santucci seemed genuinely interested in the child so she answered.

"When children are abused, it's not just the incident that harms them. There's often psychological damage. Sometimes Amy wakes up at night screaming. She gets upset when she hears a man's voice. It seems that was part of McKinney's method of attack. He would get into her bed at night. Sometimes now, in the morning, they find her sleeping under her bed." She sounded disgusted, and was.

"Damn." Santucci was lost for words for a second. "How about the perpetrator? What was his first name.....Delbert......Delbert McKinney?"

"Very good, Lieutenant. Mr. McKinney is a first offender, according to the law at least, and will probably be allowed to plead to a misdemeanor and be forced to register as a sex offender. But no jail time, if that's what you're asking."

"What!" Santucci couldn't believe it.

"The child was around lots of other people. She was living in a meth house. One of the problems with little children is that they have no vocabulary for what happened to them. They can't tell us what happened. We have to use circumstantial evidence in most cases. In this case there was just no solid proof that McKinney was the one who abused her. That's why fewer than ten percent of sex abuse complaints end up with a conviction in a criminal court."

"Lieutenant, I have to tell you something." This was as good a time as any to tell him. His expression didn't change, that was something at least. She went on when he didn't comment.

"I think one of my people is the killer." There, she said it. She had to, regardless of the consequences.

"So does everybody else. Do you have anyone specific in mind?" He got right to the point. Akin was a little shocked.

"So does everybody else?" she repeated. "I don't have anyone in mind, but the killer knows things that are in our files, almost word for word."

"That doesn't mean that it was one of your people. Don't worry Angel, we're keeping an eye on several people, and finding out some things about others," he added thoughtfully.

"Are you still going to Chicago this weekend?" He changed the subject.

"Well, yes, I am." She didn't know where this was leading.

"I may be up there myself. I may have to take a car up there for Ariano." He smiled.   "Maybe we can go out for a bite to eat or something."

A date. He was asking for a date. "Oh, sure. Maybe we could. You have my cell number?"

He nodded, smiling more broadly until she asked another question. "You said you were finding out things about people. Anything you can tell me?" She cashed in his apology for not telling her something before.

Santucci looked across the hallway where Bonnie Weatherlow was conferring with someone who looked to be an overworked public official. "Ms. Weatherlow said she was at home, sick, at the time of the child's death. She wasn't home. UPS tried to deliver a package that morning and the driver is sure there was no one home. I expect that to remain between ourselves for the moment."   He gave her a look that said many things she didn't understand.

Bonnie finished with her conference and started towards Akin and Santucci. He excused himself, stating that he would call her. Akin watched him go, not really interested in a date, but hoping he would call.

CHAPTER 36

"Can everybody hear...and see, me?" A chorus of "yeses" came out of the speakers at each location. Everyone involved in the conference was watching a flat screen segmented into eight boxes with a little face in each one. The director, in Chicago, had called the meeting to coordinate the response to the serial killings. He also needed to appear to be doing something. Every time there was another killing, his phone rang ten times as often as before.

Milo and Diego were at District 13 headquarters sitting in front of their own screen with a lens at the top. Diego was the star so he was in front of the camera. Milo was just a voice in the background, and glad of it.

The director spoke to Santucci who squirmed a little under the scrutiny. "Diego, regardless of the outcome of this conference, I would like you to run up here and give me a personal briefing on the case this weekend."

Someone had dug up some details on Santucci's past and miraculously the media had dubbed him some kind of special agent whose background and experiences gave him a unique ability to capture the serial killer. At the moment it was good PR to be seen with Lt. Santucci, the man who shunned the cameras and the limelight, even if you didn't like him. The director could barely conceal his intentions. This notoriety didn't bother Santucci's foes much; it was just that much farther for him to fall when he failed.

For the moment, Santucci was just going with the flow. It looked like a paid vacation to Chicago this weekend. Appreciate the little things. "I'll look forward to seeing you for lunch on Friday, Director. It takes about five and a half hours to run up there so I'll be ready to eat when I arrive. About 12:30, Sir?" Actually, Santucci planned to leave Thursday morning.

The director agreed, a little halfheartedly, realizing that Santucci had just thrown him a curve. It was going to be difficult to get exposure at a luncheon, but there were ways; that was a politicians' job. For the next hour the director was bombarded with more facts, ideas, and theories than Santucci could ever come close to supplying.

Milo was asked about the suspects and had to admit that they had dropped the ball on Scott Collins. "It seems that he wasn't at home when the murders were committed. We know for sure on the last one because we had our people go in and he wasn't there. We have his house wired now, but we don't know where he's been sneaking off to. And he has been sneaking off."

The director huffed and puffed for the benefit of the FBI agent who was in the lower right hand corner of the screen. He mentioned that there were now nine copycat killings which all stemmed from our case. Milo held up five fingers to Santucci off screen then closed his hand and opened it two more times. Fifteen. Santucci tried not to react.

Milo laughed, typical cynical cop, he didn't care. Santucci knew the agent in the lower corner of the screen and knew that he didn't care. Frank Wesson, in Springfield, really didn't care, and interrupted the boss' tirade suggesting that they get on with the meeting.

At one point Milo interjected a thought. "I think he's using some kind of rod or baton that fires a spike out of the end."

Santucci, sitting right next to Milo, was the first to doubt. "Sure, the wounds are a little larger in diameter than a regular ice pick you might find in a hardware store, but shooting spikes, Milo?" Santucci couldn't picture what Milo was talking about.

He started to explain, "The device would use a high tensile steel spring that could be wound with a key. It might create as much force as............."

The director thought the murder weapon was a carpenter's awl and said so, over Milo's theory, interrupting Milo and making everyone listen to a story about his father and the awls he kept in his carpenter's bag. "......I still have a couple of them around somewhere. I will try to locate them and we can use them for simulations."

Terrific idea. Milo would probably be glad to stick one in his eye.

After the meeting, Santucci and Milo headed back to the house. They both were eager to find out how school went.

"Milo, let's make Marnie Marzulo liaison officer to the Feds."

"Okay by me." Milo didn't care as long as he didn't have to be someone official.

"I'm still thinking about the ex-priest, Callahan. Why was he first? Why didn't the killer put out one of his little inflammatory messages naming Callahan. He sure did meet the criteria for one of his victims. Maybe that one was personal. If he had come out with Callahan's exploits there would have been clergymen killed by copycats, for sure. Damn this mother....." Santucci caught himself before he let out a string of curses the way Angel Akin had.

Milo caught it. "Going back to swearing?"

"No!" Santucci told himself more than anything else. Then added, "Too bad, too. I just learned a bunch of new words the other night."

Santucci went back to something he could control. "Have Marzulo get the Feds to coordinate all the data on Callahan's perps. Do you think we could get the names of all the young boys that he may have come in contact with? You know school records, stuff like that?"

"Diego, you're talking thousands of names." Milo was shaking his head, figuring.

"That's what we wanted the Feds for, Milo. So they could throw some money and personnel at us. Just tell Marnie to call me. I'll teach her how to get her way with government agencies."

CHAPTER 37

S antucci had a lot of time to think on his way to Chicago, Thursday morning. The weather was springy and clouds rumbled across the wide sky of farm country. He was driving a luxury SUV but it drove like a tank as far as he was concerned. It was one of Ariano's special jobs going overseas. The vehicle practically drove itself so he went back over some of the things that had happened before he left. Best things first.

■ ■ ■

"So how was school Michael?" Santucci had prepared himself for a gleeful assault that never came.

"Good." No eye contact.

"Did something bad happen?" Santucci was immediately alarmed. Polly spoke up for Michael.

"First day of school is a bit overwhelming, Diego. He'll catch on. It's just that there are so many new friends to meet and so much going on."

Santucci tried his best to cheer the boy up. They ordered pizza, Michael's favorite thing in the world, watched some movies, and after a while, things were fine. Michael waited until they were alone and asked Santucci a question that he knew was coming.

"Diego, you said you would know about my mom today."

"I saw her today. She looked okay. She is going to be under doctor's care for a while." Santucci was beating around the bush. Michael got specific.

"Will she be able to come home?" Michael didn't know what all the rules were but he knew what he considered normal.

Santucci stiffened his spine. "Michael, I don't think they're going to let her come home. Not like you used to have."

"I don't want it to be like we used to have," he shocked Santucci. "Even if Mom gets better Diego, we're still going to have to keep an eye on her. You don't know her like I do. Will we be able to see her sometimes?"

Santucci was choking on his words, spine wavering. "You sure will, buddy. You'll be able to see your mother all the time."

"Promise?"

"Everything I say is a promise." Santucci got a hug for that and almost broke down crying.

After Michael went to bed, Milo and Polly were in the kitchen having coffee. Santucci went down to talk to them. He refused the offer of coffee. He couldn't understand how these two could drink it so late and still sleep. He supposed they had their ways, and they apparently worked just fine.

"That's what I said. Adopted." Santucci reluctantly answered Milo's last question and the next one too.

"Even though there is an appeal process for termination of parental rights, we haven't got a chance. She violated a court order and it resulted in the death of her child. The attorney said it would be a waste of time. Believe me, I tried everything." Santucci wasn't used to being stumped.

"Diego," Polly said soothingly, "you know we would keep Michael as long as necessary, but we can't keep him for ever. He needs structure."

"I know you guys couldn't adopt him." Santucci was thoughtful. "Maybe I could adopt him." He doubted it the second he said it.

"Sh.....oot. I'm 51-years old. No wife. I live in a damn hotel. Who am I kidding? I couldn't even adopt a puppy." He was clearly disgusted with the situation.

"You're the one who says 'never say never', Diego. Get those wheels working, you'll come up with something. You always do." Milo pointed at Santucci's head when he said wheels.

■ ■ ■

His cell phone rang, breaking Santucci out of the reverie he had sunken into. He checked to make sure he was clear of other traffic and pulled it out of his coat pocket. He glanced at the display. Marnie Marzulo.

"Hi, Marnie."

"Hello, Lieutenant." She had her official voice on.

"What's going on?"

"You wanted me to call you?"

"Oh yeah. I wanted you to coordinate the federal assistance, especially as it pertains to the man who was found in the church in Missouri."

He went over everything with her. Sometimes telling her to just trust him. He thought the killer was settling an old score with the priest and told her to prove it for him.

"I'll try and catch your Advocate for you, Lieutenant," she said at one point.

"This guy is no Advocate, Marnie, don't forget it. The first person was an advocate for a murdered child. This isn't the same person. This guy has another agenda. He's just a coldblooded killer. But he has a specific reason. I just can't figure out what is it."

She could tell that Santucci wasn't talking directly to her. He was thinking out loud as much as anything else. When they were about done, she had another thought.

"Lieutenant, remember that kid who we caught fooling around with the laptop in your Corvette?"

"The one with the ratty hair?" Santucci remembered.

"Remember the disk I took away from him?"

"Yes."

"Well, I brought it home and put it on a shelf, forgot about it really. Then the other day, one of my kids picked it up and put it in our computer to see what was on it. It loaded itself onto my computer and just vanished. No information, no nothing. So my kid tried to download it again. Same thing. The only way she knew there was something on the disk was that a bunch of our hard drive got taken up. Now I can't figure out what it is or how to get my hard drive unclogged. I think that kid was trying to load this thing onto your laptop."

"I haven't noticed anything wrong with my laptop." But he was interested for some reason. "What was that kid's name? I don't think he ever told me when I asked him."

"I wrote it down so I wouldn't forget it. It was such an unusual name." There was a pause while she looked at a note. "Merlin Thistlethorn."

"Maybe we should ask Mr. Thistlethorn why his homework screwed up your computer." Santucci had another thought. "Better yet, let's find out what it is ourselves. I want you to overnight the disk to my cousin Ariano; he loves stuff like that. Get a pencil and I'll give you the information."

CHAPTER 38

The conference had been going well. On Saturday morning when Angel Akin walked into the large convention room at the Fairmont Hotel in Chicago, she was right behind Bonnie Wheatherlow. She'd been staying close to her since they had left southern Illinois. She had even juggled the roommates around so she could have a room with Bonnie. They found seats at one of the long cloth-draped tables lined with jugs of water and reading materials. Akin didn't see Santucci right away.

While the room filled up, everyone was looking around or visiting with old friends and acquaintances not seen for a while. Their table had a lot of visitors. Gerry Bennet seemed to know everybody from Chicago, mostly women.

Akin stood up to speak to a colleague that she had served on several boards with. That's when she noticed Lt. Santucci sitting quietly against the wall, looking directly at her. She realized that he had been observing her for awhile and felt a little uncomfortable, but managed to return his smile anyway. She had been lightly probing Bonnie, without any response, and hoped that Santucci wasn't there to arrest her.

She looked for Santucci during the break and couldn't find him. At the dismissal, suddenly he was there at her elbow. She spoke first, to cover her surprise.

"Where've you been all day? I saw you during the presentation, but when I looked for you at the break you were nowhere to be found," she asked in a friendly, kidding way.

Santucci sounded slightly guilty when he answered, only puzzling her more. "I'm sorry about that Angel. I didn't know if you wanted everyone to know that..... ah.....we knew each other."

So that was it, or was it? She tried to stay light. "Well, I thought that I might get you to show me a good place for lunch around here. That buffet they had was the pits."

"I'm sorry, I didn't even have any lunch. But I'd be glad to make it up to you for dinner, if you'd be interested." He smiled slyly.

"No lunch?" She asked. "What were you doing?" She tried for some information.

"This case is very complex. I can't get away from it. I thought I was coming up here for personal reasons," he smiled, "but so far I've had to meet with the director, get my picture taken with him about a thousand times, and I've been on the phone or computer constantly since yesterday when I got here."

"But why are you here? Anyone in particular you're looking for?" She returned the sly smile.

"I was wondering why Scott Collins was attending the conference," he said casually, watching her closely.

"Oh,.....Collins. The parole officer. There are representatives from every agency here, probation, DOT. I think his specialty is...was...sex offender cases. At any rate, he had to be signed up before......all this started." That seemed to satisfy him.

He changed the subject. "The seminar is really informative. I'm sorry that I missed the presentations in the afternoon. The statistics are staggering. Just to think of 500,000 sex offenders in the country. Man!" He said it like a curse.

"And at least 100,000 of them are fugitives, wanted by local or federal authorities." She recalled another frightening statistic.

"We need a national sex offender data base that can be universally added to by each state, but that would take money that is being spent on important things, commonly known as pork barrel projects."

She was bitter about some subjects. "As it is now, sexual predators abuse children and move from state to state avoiding capture and assuming new identities. And there's tens of thousands of them."

They were walking down the corridor, the crowd was thinning out. Akin realized that she didn't know where Bonnie Weatherlow had gotten to but figured if she was with Santucci, Bonnie was safe for the moment. Maybe he was after that Collins guy. When she looked around she saw Gerry Bennet approaching at a fast walk. She was stunned when he grabbed Santucci by the elbow, pulling him around, and to a stop.

"I've had it with you people! Now you're harassing my wife and children. If you can't catch your damn Advocate, quit trying to frame innocent people for it." Bennet's fists were clenched as he stared down at Santucci.

Santucci looked down at Bennet's hands and back up to his face. "Calm down Mr. Bennet. No one is framing anyone for anything."

"Don't tell me to calm down!" People had stopped and were watching the exchange. "I ought to take you apart you little....."

"Gerry! What are you saying?" Akin stepped in between the two, also looking up at Bennet.

"This is personal business, Ang." He didn't touch her but stepped around her to face Santucci once more.

"You better watch your back, Lieutenant. 'Cause I'm gonna be there some time." There wasn't as much force behind this statement as he had started with, but he had apparently decided to say something stupid and followed through with it.

Santucci's expression didn't change but his voice got hard and low. Like a growl. "Mr. Bennet, don't get personal with me, sir. You don't want me as your enemy. You don't want me thinking bad thoughts about you. Believe me." The last was like a hypnotic suggestion.

Bennet was stunned into silence by the quiet force of the statement.

Santucci smiled in a very friendly way, his voice changing from a deadly chill to a soothing smoothness. "Now we'll just pretend this conversation never happened, don't you think?"

He turned to Dr. Akin, took her hand and led her away without another word, as though they had just passed a few pleasant moments with a friend. There was never a dull moment around this guy.

CHAPTER 39

"What the hell is this?" Angel Akin was smiling, but she clearly wanted an answer before getting into the big black vehicle. Not a car, not a truck, but not an SUV either. The roof was clear glass so she could see the tucked and rolled leather seats like the ones in the squad car, but there was a lot more in this thing. The back seat looked like a limousine. It had shining wood panels with a glass partition separating it from the front compartment.

"It's one of Ariano's specials. We're delivering it for shipment overseas." He answered as though it was no big deal. She didn't press it, hiked up her best skirt and climbed in. She'd been in enough pickup trucks, often times dressed up, and this thing was nothing but a fancy pickup to her.

Santucci went around and climbed in behind the wheel. The way he pulled himself up into the cab showed that he was more comfortable sliding behind the wheel of an old Stingray.

"Don't things go overseas from the coast?" she asked.

"Port of Chicago. This baby is going out UPS; Ariano's clients can afford it."

"What's so different about this thing?"

They pulled smoothly out into traffic, oncoming vehicles making room for them in downtown Chicago traffic lanes.

"Look at your cell phone," he prompted.

She got it out of her purse and looked.

"See how many bars you have on your signal strength indicator."

She looked at the corner of the screen. "Wow, we don't have signal strength like this down south. Heck, I didn't even know there were that many bars on this thing."

Santucci touched the computer screen in the dash board. All the bars on Akin's phone disappeared at the same time.

"What happened?" She looked over at him.

"This vehicle has cell phone dampening technology."

She was still looking at her phone. "What for? So no one can call you?"

"Roadside bombs are most often detonated by cell phones. It also has G.P.S., infra-red, the whole thing is bullet proof, you name it," he said, looking over at her.

She got it. "Who's this thing for anyway?"

"I could find out. But I don't really know. Anonymity is also for sale. "

"Doesn't the government control that stuff? Why don't they buy it from the government?"

"Our vehicles only come with the things that are ordered. No bugs in the woodwork." She looked at him and he winked.

"Check this out." He touched the screen again, running his finger down. The roof darkened and the windows began to darken also. "Polarized."

"Cool, Santucci, we gonna park by the lake?"

He looked at her, a little surprised.

"I had a boyfriend from Chicago once," she smiled slyly.

He laughed. "What are you hungry for? How 'bout sushi?"

"Yuck," she answered, with sound effects.

"Well, what's your favorite?"

"Mexican," she said, smiling knowingly.

"Well, you're with the right Mexican for Mexican." They were waiting at a light. "What are you in the mood for? Good food. Or ambiance?"

"I thought French food came with ambiance. How about good food?"

He headed west and south from the downtown area and soon they were in one of the neighborhoods of Chicago. There were tall red brick buildings with stores at the street level. A lot of Spanish wording on the signs that were everywhere.

Santucci finally pulled up in front of a church, parking in a bus stop. When she looked up at the threatening signs, *Tow Zone/No Parking/Bus Stop*, that were attached to the post next to them, Santucci waved it away. This was Chicago.

"We're not going far. This thing would probably bite anyone that tried to tow it anyway." They got out. Akin looked up to the towering church spire then back to Santucci.

He answered her question before she asked it. "In this church is the shrine of St. Jude Thaddeus, the patron saint of hopeless causes," he said, with a bit of awe in his voice.

"St. Jude?" she asked.

"He did a big favor for Danny Thomas once." Santucci thought of how the favor was repaid, namely St. Jude's Hospital for Children.

"Are we here to ask for a favor?" Akin was serious and a little impressed.

"You know, I'm not sure. When you wanted good food, I thought of this place, but not to visit the shrine. My grandmother and mother used to come here and pray for every ailment that befell the family." He was thoughtful for a moment. "I didn't think this was a hopeless case, but here I am standing in front of the place. Well, let's eat first and see if we get any inspiration."

"Eat? Where are we going to eat? At the rectory?" She gestured toward the building next to the church, with the word *Rectory* over the doorway.

"No, over there." He pointed to a little woman who was standing behind two little metal carts that were on the sidewalk, at the curb, down in front of the big wooden doors of the church.

"That little woman makes the best Mexican food in the city of Chicago. You can take my word for it."

Akin smiled at him but she wasn't convinced.

Santucci spoke to the woman in Spanish for a moment. It was obvious that part of the conversation involved Akin because the little woman smiled at her and nodded as if in introduction. Then he turned to Akin. "Hot?" he asked, smiling

"The hotter the better," she said defiantly.

Santucci looked at the little woman who understood English well enough. *"Dos 'lingua, salsa verdi. Por favor'"*

The woman quickly produced two handmade tortillas, deftly scooped some meat onto them and doused them with a green sauce. Santucci handed one to Akin and touched his to hers as if in a toast.

She smiled and took the challenge. It was the most delicious thing she had ever tasted in her life, and the hottest. It wasn't hot right away, it sort of snuck up on you. There was only one thing to do in a case like that, keep shoveling. They had two more, each, after Santucci introduced her to the little boy who sold the lemonade that was the antidote to the hot green chili sauce.

Santucci put his fingers in the woman's apron. She looked down and started to protest but he would hear none of it and she relented easily. They'd done this before. Santucci started towards the parked vehicle.

"I figured out the green sauce," she said, "but what is *lingua*?"

He looked at her as if deciding whether to tell her or not, then finally said, "Tongue."

"Eeeeuuu...." She was sorry she asked. "Maybe I should have tried the sushi."

"Really?" he asked.

"No," she smiled sincerely, "that was the best taco I ever had. Best three tacos I ever had," she corrected. Then she changed the subject.

"Aren't you going to stop in and ask for your favor?" She looked up at the gigantic red brick edifice.

"I don't consider this a hopeless case." he said thoughtfully. "You don't want to waste favors on little things."

She just looked at him. He didn't consider this a hopeless case. She tried to draw some solace from the thought. There wasn't much.

Then he changed his mind. "But it never hurts to pay your respects, I guess. Let's go in for a second."

CHAPTER 40

S he followed him up the long flight of steps. He held the big door for her. It seemed to open easily despite its immense size. The inside of the church was beautiful and warm. Akin wasn't Catholic so she was trying to absorb as many things as possible. Tall stained glass windows, statues, and frescos lined the walls. The wood was a soft color. The three altars were very ornate, with a choir practicing on the far one. Santucci walked up to a niche in the left wall and knelt down for a second, seemed to say a short prayer, then put something in a metal box. He came back to where she had stopped to look around.

"That didn't take long." she said when they were back outside.

"I'm not very religious but it never hurts to show a little respect." He held the car door for her, another thing she had gotten used to easily.

"So what do you want to do now? This is Chicago." He said it as though it encompassed all things.

"Well, as good as it was, dinner was kind of quick. I guess we have time to do something. What do you suggest." She passed the ball back to him.

His phone rang. "Let's see, that may be something." He dug around in his coat pocket and flipped the phone open.

"Why, hello........yes, Mickey, I did call you. Right now though, I am entertaining a friend from out of town and we're looking for something to do."

Santucci looked over at Akin. "You like BB King?"

"BB King? Well yeah." She wondered if there were people who didn't.

"Park Place? Okay, Mick. We'll be there." He put the phone away.

"I was looking through the paper. I didn't see a BB King concert advertised," she commented as they headed north.

"It's a private party, a fund-raiser," he supplied by way of an answer while he raced through the streets. Akin was glad he knew where he was going because it was all a blur to her.

The party was across the street from a park in a low profile building that looked as though it had been a small theater years ago. It had rained but the street was alive with people in a "Saturday Night" mood. Once inside the glass doors they were in a lobby that was packed with people trying to get through another set of glass doors. Santucci waved at someone inside the club and soon the crowd parted and they were ushered in.

The private party had about 500 guests. There was a wide stage surrounded with comfortable seating and a long bar, packed with revelers. There were beautiful women, who looked like people would give them money for any reason, walking around with clear canisters that were full of money. They could hardly take a step before someone else was stuffing bills in the slot on the top.

Santucci smiled back at the first girl who approached and put some money in the can. Akin was obviously just along for the ride, but it was fun and a bit overwhelming. Michael "Mickey" Doohan was their host and also the life of the party. He wouldn't let them order a drink or pay for anything, insisting on opening champagne for them. Angel knew it was a Dom Pérignon but would have liked a beer to go with her tacos.

"I could have gone for a beer," Santucci said matching her thought.

"Me too," she smiled. "How do these people raise so much money?" She gestured towards the canisters that were everywhere, packed with money.

"All you need is a good cause and a Scotsman like Mickey Doohan," Santucci answered. "I was thinking about what you said regarding a children's center and I thought...."

"Diego, come on! Tell me! Where do you find all these beautiful women?" Mickey slapped Santucci on the back and ogled Akin. He was way ahead of them on the champagne. Akin smiled at him.

"She's my doctor, Mick." Strange thing for him to say but Akin kept smiling.

"Doctor! I need an examination right away. I need you to get to work on me, Doc!" He grabbed his chest for emphasis.

"She's a child psychologist, Mickey," Santucci told him.

"All the better.   I'm working on my second childhood and if I ain't nuts I don't know who is," he laughed heartily.

"I have to agree with you on that," Santucci and Akin laughed with him.

A beautiful sound, that could only be Lucille, came from the stage, taking everyone's attention. When she stopped for a moment, BB King's voice came in behind her; he never sang over Lucille. "Everyday.................... Everyday, I have the blues...."

"Tell me about it," Akin thought, sipping her bubbles and sitting back to enjoy the show.

CHAPTER 41

They only stayed for a few songs, which was fine with Akin; the bubbles and the atmosphere were things she couldn't take for long. Once Santucci had her in the vehicle, he tipped the valet and pulled away from the club, which was still going strong, the lobby still packed with people.

"Is Mickey one of 'da boys?'" she asked, trying the Chicago accent.

He shook his head. "One of "the boys?" I told you that "the boys" were criminals. We don't hang around with criminals, Angel. Mickey is just a rich guy who I did a favor for when he wasn't rich."

"What kind of favor?" she smiled wryly.

"He was about to get dead and I got him out of it."

"That doesn't sound like anything criminal was going on." She didn't wait for a comment. "How did he get rich after you kept him from getting dead?"

"He doesn't look it, but he's a computer geek. Figured out how to double the capacity on a microchip, or something like that, and made a billion. He and Ariano have conversations about things that haven't been conceived yet all the time. I stay out of it."

"It's getting late; back to the hotel?" Santucci asked, reading her mind and turning down a side street.

They were approaching an intersection. The street was wet. The branches of the trees hanging with new growth, and rain drops, lit only by the beams of their headlights, created a tunnel-like effect bordered with parked cars that lined both sides. The only break in the tunnel was at the upcoming cross street.

Santucci was rolling slowly. Suddenly, from their right, a frightened young man ran into the light of their headlights and stopped, looking at them as if for a place of refuge. He was breathing heavily, had obviously been running for a while. Seeing nothing but lights, and with no place to hide, a glance back toward the way he had come spurred the boy on across their path and down the side street to the left. The look on his face alerted both Santucci and Akin that the boy was in a panic.

Right after the first boy, another one came loping along, a calm, satisfied look on his face. He didn't bother to look into the headlights, not wanting to lose sight of his prey. He continued on after the first boy.

Still rolling, they were almost to the intersection, when they observed another young man come from their right, following the first two. As he passed the light of their beams, Santucci and Akin saw that, down along the side of his leg, the third boy was trying to conceal a long-bladed knife. He gave them but a glance, as if to make sure there were no lights on top of their vehicle, and proceeded after the pair.

The vehicle was in the intersection now, still rolling. Down the side street they could see that the first, panicked boy, his white-shirted chest shoved out, was now being firmly held from behind by the second boy. They were a few car lengths down, under a street light, and Santucci and Akin could see the action clearly.

The third boy was running towards the frozen pair now. His left arm, holding the knife, was pulled back. He was preparing to thrust the blade into the panicked boy using all the force he could muster.

"Diego! Do something!" Akin cried out.

Santucci hit the door lock and opened his car door. They were almost across the intersection, still rolling slowly. Then he hollered, in his most official voice, "Stop! Police Officers!" He used his other hand to beep the horn, only it was a police siren that wailed in the night.

The knife was on its way. It was only the quick reflexes of the wielder that stopped it a scant inch from the stomach of the first boy. The scene froze for a second, the knife hanging in the air. Then the first boy gave one last desperate effort and broke away from his captor. He ran towards Santucci and Akin; the two attackers were still frozen in place.

Santucci continued to roll into the next block. The frightened boy, hope in his face now, ran after the vehicle. Santucci still had his door open; he looked back at the boy who was now chasing them.

"Hey man! Dem guys were gonna stab me!" he called out to Santucci.

"I know." Santucci answered, still rolling. There was no sign of the two attackers.

"Ain't you gonna stop?" the boy asked.

"I just saved you, and now you want me to give you a ride?" Santucci stated.

The boy realized that it wasn't a real police vehicle that had happened by to save his life. In that split second he turned left and disappeared into the alley without a word of thanks.

"Diego! Holy-shit! Wow!" she screamed. "Aren't we gonna stop?"

"The car may be bullet proof, but we aren't." He smiled at her enthusiasm. "We'll just call it in and let them send a car around. Okay?"

Akin was a little dismayed but realized that they couldn't go around playing police too much.

After he made the call, and the adrenaline rush had subsided a bit, she said, "So what was that Santucci, a Chicago-style wolves and sheep story?"

"Woof," said the sheepdog.

CHAPTER 42

They were cruising south on Lake Shore Drive. A locally famous song of the same name came on the radio just as they merged into traffic. It was really beautiful, for a city. Akin looked at the tall buildings, all lit up, people everywhere going someplace in a hurry, and figured that Chicago stayed awake pretty much all night on a Saturday, but she couldn't. They had just been chatting when she realized that they were talking about sex.

"What did you say?" she asked, bringing herself back to reality.

"What?" he asked.

"Are we talking about sex?" She knew that this guy was slick but couldn't understand how he could slide so smoothly around a subject like that.

"You brought it up." He was totally innocent. She had to think for a second.

"All right." You want to talk about sex, she thought, "Let me ask you a question."

He didn't say no.

"When was the first time you had sex?"

Bet he wished he had said "no" now. He looked over at her, weighing the question.

"A long time ago." That wasn't an answer. She waited.

"Do you mean when did I first have sex?"

She thought the question was clear and continued to wait.

"Well, you see," He put his finger in his collar and stretched it unnecessarily. "When I was a kid, my cousin and I used to stay together on a weekend night when our parents would go out. And we had a girl cousin who used to babysit for us."

She continued to listen without comment or prompt.

He continued trying to explain something that he had probably never had to talk about before. "She sort of showed us how everything worked. Of course we were too young to do much but..."

"And when you were in high school, did you date the other girls in the class? Did you go to the prom?" She knew she was on to something.

"Well, the girl I was going out with at the time... she was a little older, she had her own apartment. We didn't get into school stuff. I don't know why." He was hesitating.

"And you've never been married? No children?" She completed her thought.

"Well, no," he said flatly.

"Diego," she softened her voice, "Think about it. Mickey Doohan asked where you found all the beautiful women. They've always found you. You've never had a problem with women. Dating older ones when you were young. Younger ones when you got older."

He wasn't commenting now, so she went on. "For a boy to be introduced to sex at such a young age isn't as traumatic as it is for a girl, but face it, you were abused by your older female cousin, and it has affected your ability to have a meaningful relationship."

She didn't want to complete the thought, at least not out loud. "You're not going to be able to adopt Michael with a background like that."

"I couldn't adopt Michael," he said, spurred out of his thoughts.

"That's what I said." She didn't look over at him.

"The next time you want to ask me a question before we go to bed, Angel, the answer is NO!" he stated definitely.

She looked over at him now. "Wait a second. Who said anything about going to bed?" She wondered if he could tell how long it had been for her. Probably to the day.

"Well, I didn't," he said, making it sound as though it were her idea again. It may have been a thought, but that's all it was going to be.

"Diego," she softened a little, "you are a sexually active person. I'm not. There are too many things going around these days to have casual sex anymore."

"Well," he said, "there are ways..."

"Are you talking about using 'protection'?" She made little quotes in the air with her fingers.

"Well, there's nothing wrong with being safe." Now he was the safe one.

She wasn't going for it. "Let me tell you something, Santucci. I like unprotected sex." Her voice had an edge to it. It had been a long time. "Not only that, but I think sex is something that is an act of love, not just exercise. You know how I exercise."

He only nodded thoughtfully. She didn't have to say more. His phone rang, breaking the tension. He spoke for a moment and told the caller he'd get back to him.

"Angel, reach in the back seat and get my laptop, will you?"

She looked to him for more information; she wasn't moving.

"There's been another Advocate slaying. Here in Chicago."

She knew the implications immediately and reached for the leather case. "Open it up and go online. I have several sites marked that should have the message playing."

She pulled out the machine and with practiced ease soon had it working. "You know, I have the same model but my laptop is nowhere near as fast as this one," she commented. "In fact, mine seems to be slower lately."

"Ariano has been tinkering with it. I'm surprised it doesn't fly," Santucci said, looking over at her.

Akin was looking at the screen that had popped up on Santucci's computer. It was a grainy picture of what looked like a Wal-Mart store's checkout section.

Santucci noticed and answered her question before she asked it. "That's the guy."

"The guy?"

"Well, that's the picture from a Wal-Mart security camera of the guy who bought the cell phone that the Advocate's calls are coming from. We think he's the guy."

She looked at the picture more closely now. It was a man standing at one of the self-checking stations. The problem with the picture was that Wal-Mart wanted to keep an eye on the computer screen as the customer checked out his items. The guy had his back to the camera lens.

"Would have been nice if he had looked into the camera," she commented.

Santucci just grunted agreement. "He knew he was being filmed. Went in and out of the store through the garden center door. No camera. By the time we figured out which store he bought the phone in, the money he used was co-mingled and this was the only picture we had." He wasn't happy about anything he had just said.

She had another thought. "If you knew he was a white male, why all the interest in Bonnie and the others in my office and parole/probation?"

"He's got to be getting inside information somehow. There are theories that have two people working together on this. It's happened before," he commented, sounding as though he didn't believe it.

Akin had been staring at the figure; he seemed familiar somehow. Tall, well built, wearing jeans and a dark jacket. Red baseball cap, probably St. Louis Cardinals. There were only thousands upon thousands of those around southern Illinois. Still.

"Do you mind if I e-mail this to myself?" she asked.

"If you mail me the screen saver site for the missing children."

She agreed gladly and soon had one of the web sites with the Advocate's latest message playing. Santucci pulled off the drive onto a side street and stopped so they could both hear it. The non-gender computerized voice was clear.

I AM THE ADVOCATE........TONIGHT MORE CHILDREN WILL BE SAFE BECAUSE I HAVE REMOVED TWO MORE MONSTERS FROM OUR COMMUNITY. RALPH CONRIED WAS WANTED IN INDIANA FOR RAPING THE CHILDREN OF HIS GIRLFRIEND. HE WAS ALSO WANTED FOR PREDATORY SEXUAL ABUSE OF THE CHILDREN OF A WOMAN HE WAS ENGAGED TO IN OHIO FIVE YEARS AGO. ALTHOUGH THE POLICE IN TWO STATES WERE LOOKING FOR THIS MAN, HE JUST MOVED TO ANOTHER STATE AND TOOK UP WITH ANOTHER WOMAN AND WAS SOON MOLESTING HER CHILDREN. THE POLICE COULDN'T FIND THIS MAN. DECENT PEOPLE HAVE TO DO THEIR JOBS FOR THEM. THE POLICE CAN FIND THIS FIEND'S BODY ON THE LAKEFRONT AT 31ST STREET. THE OTHER CHILD RAPIST WHO WAS DISPATCHED TONIGHT WAS ALONZO DUNCAN. HE WAS RELEASED FROM PRISON AND AWARDED A NEW TRIAL, AFTER BEING FOUND GUILTY OF RAPING TWO LITTLE GIRLS WHILE THEY WERE ON THEIR WAY HOME, BY A COURT SYSTEM WHICH DOES NOT WORK AND ALLOWS THESE PREDATORS TO REPEAT THEIR CRIMES OVER AND OVER. I URGE ALL DECENT PEOPLE TO PROTECT OUR CHILDREN.

They were soon back at the hotel where Akin was staying. Santucci pulled up in front. "Sorry we'll have to cut our conversation short, Angel. Next time maybe I'll ask you a few personal questions." He smiled wryly.

She got the message but before she got out of the truck/thing she moved towards him and kissed him. And not a peck. She wasn't a prude. She just had a different agenda. He seemed a little startled, but was smiling and shaking his head when she looked back before she went through the hotel doors.

CHAPTER 43

H e was transfixed by the soft lapping waves of the black Lake Michigan water. He could remember swimming in that water as a child. It was always cold. The scene behind him was well lighted, but the vast lake swallowed the flood light easily.

The Chicago Police Crime Lab was in charge and had the scene covered expertly. They said it was a fortunate coincidence to have the lead state investigator on the case here in Chicago when the serial killer had claimed his next victims. They didn't say that Santucci probably brought the killer up with him from southern Illinois. They didn't have to say it.

His phone rang, breaking his reverie. He looked at the lighted display and answered it.

"Hi, Angel. What's happening?"

"Diego," she sounded worried, which worried him. "Bonnie isn't here. I don't think she even came back to the room."

He was relieved. "Don't worry."

"Don't worry?" Her voice had that edge. "But you said...."

"Angel. Trust me and don't worry." He emphasized it. Then he had another thought. "Can you have Bonnie and Gerry Bennet in your office Monday afternoon?"

"Yes." She sounded skeptical. "Why do you want those two?"

"Angel, I'm sorry. I've got Milo on the other line. Can you do that for me?"

She reluctantly said she would and he answered the incoming call, feeling as though he should have told her more.

"Milo. Tell me something, anything." He had sand in his shoes and his attitude was just as gritty.

"The killer screwed up." Sounded good; Santucci waited. Milo went on after there was no comment.

"Alonzo Duncan was an innocent man."

That got a response from Santucci. "What about Conried? Was he innocent too?" Santucci's tone was sarcastic; he was frustrated, and regretted it immediately.

"No. Conreid was a scumbag who attached himself to women so he could molest their children." It was clear that Milo wasn't sorry Conried had bought it. "But Duncan is a whole different story. He was identified as a predator by two girls who had gone to a gang party where they were forbidden to go, had gotten raped by the gang members and then said they had gotten attacked in the park by a black man. When they picked Alonzo Duncan up and put him in a lineup the first girl signaled 'number three' to her friend after coming out of the viewing room. The other girl identified Duncan and he went to prison. He served three years out of a 25-year sentence, then one of the girls told someone what they had done. Soon, real DNA tests were done, the girls confessed, and they had no choice but to release Duncan. The new trial was just a formality."

"Our killer screwed up." Santucci repeated.

"That's what I said."

"So he comes up here with the people in the convention. He wants the people from southern Illinois to be solid suspects. He's got to have another agenda. He's trying to cover something up," Santucci mused to himself as much as to Milo.

"What about Conried?" he asked finally. "How did he find Conried?"

"He did what he said. He did a better job than the police." Milo wasn't happy about this admission. "A call came into the DCFS Child Abuse Hotline. A woman stated that Ralph Conried was at a south side address and that he was wanted for sex crimes in another state. They sent a patrol car out to the address and there was no answer when they knocked on the door." Milo didn't say that they blew the job off.

Santucci grunted, understanding.

Milo had more. "Later, the same woman called back and identified herself as the sister of Conried's girlfriend and stated that Conried had been molesting her niece and nephew and that the mother and children were at her house. DCFS assigned a field investigator who went to the house and supposedly notified the police again, after she interviewed the family. Well, sometime in there while all that ball-dropping was going on, Conried went missing and got himself dead." Clear and concise, never quite.

"The bastard is monitoring everything," he paused to apologize to no one for swearing. "Damn." Another pause, then he gave up. "He is better than us. I'm flying out of here tonight. Can you pick me up at the airport?" Santucci was disgusted down to his shoes, which were full of sand.

CHAPTER 44

"This is a black mark for our state, gentlemen. And if there is anyone that thinks he's going to get in on this media circus by committing a copycat killing I want him prosecuted to the fullest extent of the law. Now that the Advocate is loose in Chicago, I want the CPD to have full access to every detail in the case. Maybe they can catch this maniac." That was apparently all the governor had to say because he just got up from the chair and was soon out of camera range. Santucci knew that he was the target of everyone's pointed finger. He didn't care. He deserved it. He knew.

He half listened to the director, upper left corner of the screen today, as he repeated the governor's words and added a few more of his own implied threats. When the meeting ended Santucci headed for the DCFS office and his meeting with Bonnie Weatherlow and Gerry Bennet. So far it had been a bad day and didn't look to be improving any.

Angel Akin didn't improve it any with the look she gave him when he came in. He was cordial and professional and got right to the point.

"Ms. Weatherlow, Mr. Bennet," Santucci addressed them directly. There had been no hellos or handshaking. Looking nervous, Bonnie sat as far from the door as she could get. Gerry Bennet waited until Santucci sat and moved to the chair directly across from him. Then he just stared a hole into Santucci, not making him uncomfortable at all. These two were just addressing their own apprehensions in their own ways.

"The State of Illinois has gone through a lot of time and effort to find out about you two."

"You don't know nothing about...." Bennet was on his feet, fist clenched again.

"I've got pictures, Gerry. Now sit down and quit trying to make me angry." Santucci's look and comment deflated the big man who sat down with a resigned sigh. Bonnie was biting on a piece of tissue, not wanting to hear more.

"Ms. Weatherlow. You told police that you were home sick on the day of the first murder. We know that you were not there. I'm not saying we think it. Everything I am telling you two is a fact that can be corroborated. So let me talk and we can get through this faster."

"You were with Mr. Bennet that day. You were with him in his room in Chicago when the murders were committed over the weekend. You two people have been lying to the police in a very serious matter to cover up an affair." Santucci looked over to Akin, who had been sitting in the corner trying to be inconspicuous, and smiled to himself at the calm expression she was fighting to maintain.

When they were smart enough not to start arguing with him or denying his accusations, Santucci went on, just wanting to get it over with, but needing to say a thing or two before he was through with them.

"You people are supposed to be the guardians of our families. You are the ones who decide if a person is a fit parent. You have the power to take children away from their mothers and fathers. Your conduct is disgraceful. You both have spouses and children. I think you're both hypocrites.

"There will not be any charges or further involvement by our office..." Gerry Bennet started to say something, a look of contrition had been born on his face.

"Don't say anything, Mr. Bennet." Santucci held up his hand. "We will not involve ourselves in your affair but if we are contacted by attorneys for your wife or her husband, the information will be released to them. And the photos, video and audio. I suggest you both take steps to solidify your situations."

They realized that they were dismissed and filed from the room without comment. Akin held back to talk to Santucci.

She gave him a fake punch to the arm, smiling, happy. "You rat. Why didn't you tell me they were fooling around together?"

"I wanted to see the expression on your face."

She punched him harder, but he moved before it connected. Smiling her biggest smile she said, "You have to buy me dinner then."

"All right. When?" he asked.

"I eat every day. Tonight's as good as any."

When he didn't say no, she added. "And bring Michael, we'll get a pizza."

So it was going to be that kind of date, Santucci thought. Then, when he thought about bringing Michael, he realized that he could spend time with the boy and Akin together. He started to think that this might be a really good idea.

CHAPTER 45

The next week was different. They went out three nights that week, twice with Michael, and settled into a sort of close, non-sexual, relationship. And there were no murders. The media speculated the killer had stopped because he had killed an innocent man. The vigilantes were losing their short-lived popularity. There were discussions about the *Rule of Law*. The copycat murders had stopped or were not being reported. One thing for sure, no one was calling themselves the Advocate any longer.

Early in the following week Santucci got a call from Marnie Marzulo.

"Lieutenant." He couldn't get her to call him Diego. "I have the names of all the boys of the target ages who may have had contact with Father Callahan. Well, not all of them, but a frightfully great number."

"Ex-father Callahan," he corrected.

"If you mean 'ex' like in dead, I agree with you. What a monster. It's incredible how much damage one pedophile can do. You know what he used to say to the boys while he was sodomizing them?" It had shaken her faith.

"Please, Marnie, don't tell me." He was serious.

"Okay." She let him off the hook. "What do you want me to do with this file?"

"Can you e-mail it to me?" he asked.

"It's a big file. Thousands of names."

"I've got a few extra boards in my machine; I can hold it."

"Okay, but it may take a while to download." She had another thought. "What ever happened to that disk from the hippie kid?"

"Ariano sent me a vague message. I gather it's something big. But what's big to him probably won't mean anything to us. We'll see soon, if I know him. Once he's into something that interests him, he doesn't sleep until he unravels it."

Milo was on the other line so he signed off with Marzulo.

"Bad news," was all Milo said.

Santucci broke his rule and asked what it was. "Okay, tell me."

"Scott Collins is addicted to gambling."

"What? What does that have to do with anything?"

"The surveillance team in Chicago followed him to a gambling boat. He was there during the murders. Well, during one of them for sure. So I contacted our people down at the gambling boat in southern Illinois."

"We have 'people' at the gambling boat in southern Illinois?" Santucci asked.

"Well....not 'we,'" Milo admitted sheepishly.

"Just tell me." Santucci's last suspect was about to slip the net.

"The guy is there constantly. On video every time. On the morning of the first killing. Later, when he sneaked out of his house during one of the serial killings, he was going to the boat. He has a buddy on the next street that he was sneaking out with. They save money that way. The gambling boat owns his house. His credit card debt is around a 100 grand."

"Hell, he would have been better off in prison." Santucci was disgusted, a feeling that he couldn't quite shake lately. He had another call and told Milo to report the findings to Springfield.

"Michael." His mood improved immediately.

"Diego. Can we go for pizza tonight?"

"All you ever want to eat is pizza."

"I like pizza." Michael said. Santucci had to agree with him but didn't say so.

"Are you angry?" the boy asked.

"No. We can go for pizza if you'd like," Santucci said.

"I don't mean about the pizza." He didn't say "silly". "Are you angry because you can't find the bad man?"

This kid amazed him continuously. "I'm not angry, Michael. I'm just a little upset because something is going to happen and I can't figure out what it is."

"You just have to keep trying, Diego." Sound advice from a five-year-old. "I remember when I couldn't read. But I kept on trying and now I can. See?"

"Yes. Thank you." Santucci was speechless yet again.

"Can Doctor Angel come with us for pizza?"

"Yes. Thank you."

CHAPTER 46

Two more weeks went by, and no killings. But that didn't mean anything to Santucci. He had forced himself to take Thursday and Friday off to shake off a little stress but had done nothing but stare at his computer until his eyes hurt. He felt like a mailman who took a long walk on his day off.

Santucci had been reading the names of Father Callahan's potential and actual victims for hours. He didn't have to because the Feds were cross-referencing the names with every database available. Marzulo had explained it to him. She was really excited about how everything was done, especially how they were set up to track the killer's cell phone when he turned it on. This was all new to her. Santucci didn't care about anything but catching him. He had to keep trying.

He picked up his cell phone and made a call, letting his computer screen switch to the Wal-Mart scene of the back of the killer at the checkout station, his favorite wallpaper. It rang a few times but he knew his cousin didn't sleep.

"Ariano. Did you find out what that disk was for?" He was getting desperate.

"*Si, Amigo.......*" A string of words followed so swiftly that Santucci couldn't understand him. When he got excited, Ariano started thinking in Spanish. Santucci couldn't and stopped him.

"English, please." He waited, knowing that frustrated his cousin.

"Cousin, where did you get this disk?" He knew how to frustrate Santucci also. Answer a question with a question.

"Come on, Ariano!"

"All right." He couldn't contain his excitement any longer even for the satisfaction of giving Santucci a hard time. "This disk loads a program onto a computer which allows the controller, the guy who sabotages you, to access anything on your computer."

"They already have stuff like that, don't they?" Santucci thought he knew enough to at least talk with geeks like Ariano and Mickey Doohan.

"Not like this. This is invisible. It goes right past virus protection. If I didn't have the disk I wouldn't believe it was possible. And it infects other computers and allows the saboteur to monitor anything on those computers too. It's ingenious. Whoever wrote this calls it the 'Chameleon.'"

"I'm getting tired of clever titles," Santucci sighed.

"We could make a lot of money with this, *Amigo*. I was just going to call Mickey when you called. He's gonna jump out of his pants when he sees this."

"Don't tell any body about it. It's evidence in a murder case." Santucci's mind was finally racing after something. "No. Tell me. Tell me everything you can about it. Then send it to me overnight."

Santucci had another thought. "And don't copy it!"

"No.......no I won't." Too late.

Santucci listened for a while, asking questions. Then he gave Ariano more instructions and disconnected the call, arrowing down his phone book list until he found the name he wanted for the next call. His mind was racing; this was it, he hoped.

Marnie Marzulo came onto the line sounding a little groggy. Santucci realized that it was the middle of the night, actually Friday morning.

"I'm sorry, Marnie." He started with an apology. "What was the name of the kid with the disk?"

She sighed and groaned a bit, thinking. "Lieutenant, do you know what time it is?" She asked, to give her mind a little time to wake up, plus she was a little pissed.

"Uh...3:23." He said matter-of-factly.

She figured it must be important so she just tried to concentrate; maybe if she remembered he'd let her go back to sleep.   "Merl....Merlin Thistlethorn," she finally said with some satisfaction.

"We have to find that kid, and I mean now. That disk is the connection we've been looking for. Ariano said he's checked a bunch of law enforcement and government Web sites and the program is on all of them. The program lets the kid go anywhere he wants and look at anything he wants. And I'll bet when Ariano checks the DCFS computer network, it's going to be on there too."

Marzulo groaned again, but she was awake now. "The kid lives just off campus. We'll have a campus cop go by there and pick him up. Are you and Sergeant-Major Kratochvil coming down?"

"Uh...yes, I'll go downstairs and get him up." Santucci realized that even the best house guest got to be a pain sooner or later, especially if he woke you up in the middle of the morning.

CHAPTER 47

"I want every copper in southern Illinois to have a picture of this kid imprinted on his mind, not just inside his hat," Santucci said, to no one in particular.

Santucci was disgusted again. He was in Thistlethorn's living room which was also apparently a sophisticated techno-geek's laboratory. There was sure enough junk in there. When the campus police had arrived, they had found the door wide open. Going in, without a warrant or permission, they had heard their radio transmissions emanating from loudspeakers mounted around the room. Thistlethorn had heard them coming and beat it.

"He can monitor every police band that there is." Marzulo was impressed with the technology in the room. "There must be a couple of antennas in the attic of this building."

"Milo, get me warrants for this place. I want every piece of equipment and every stick of furniture out of here by noon and on its way to Springfield."

Milo knew Santucci was hot but didn't care. "Diego, if we start disconnecting things around here, we may lose evidence of what it was all capable of."

"Sorry, Milo. Do what you want with it, but I want an army around this place. No one in or out without extreme scrutiny. This kid has that program on enough government computers to go to jail for a thousand years now." He was thoughtful for a second.

"If he doesn't get the death penalty first." Santucci didn't like it for some reason. His mind kept going back to the picture of the checkout station at Wal-Mart. Although Thistlethorn was the right size, he had too much hair to squeeze it all under a ball cap, if he still had the hair. Santucci left the room to the experts and looked around the house. The kid slept on a dirty mattress on the floor, no sheets, just a blanket and a striped tick pillow. He didn't have much furniture, just cement blocks with boards for shelves. He spent his money on technology. There were computers, monitors, stuff he couldn't begin to understand and computer disks by the thousands. It was going to take the lab months to figure it all out.

In the kitchen he found something else that the kid spent money on. There was a coffee grinder and a small bag of coffee beans, Blue Mountain coffee, from Jamaica. It was the most expensive, and actually the best-tasting, coffee in the world.

"Milo, where was that internet coffee shop where the first message was e-mailed from?" he asked.

"Clear over on the other side of town," Milo said, dismissing any connection.

"I'm gonna go for coffee."

He got the directions and told Milo to call him when they found the kid. There was a dragnet out the likes of nothing ever seen in southern Illinois before. It wouldn't be long. They had his cell phone number and were set up to track the signal, although the kid had it turned off. His vehicle and personal description were being broadcast over every police radio within 100 miles. They were prepared to expand the perimeter if necessary.

When Santucci got out of his car, actually he was driving Milo's son's little compact car, he heard a helicopter go over. He just sighed and went into the little corner shop. Inside the *Caff & net* the tables were mostly empty at this early hour. Santucci went up to the counter and asked the clerk if he had any Blue Mountain coffee.

"We don't grind it man, but we sell it." The clerk was really friendly. "The coffee we have this morning is Organic Sumatran. Shade grown," he added, as though that made it.

Santucci tried not to notice the studs the clerk had sticking out of his face, eyebrows, lips, tongue and one that went through the bridge of his nose. His hair was shaved on the sides with the center long and spiked with hair gel. There was a lot of metal on this kid, around his neck, around his wrists and several rings on odd fingers. It must take him a lot of time to get ready for work, Santucci figured.

"Let me have a cup of the.........what you said, and a package of the Blue Mountain," Santucci asked. The clerk got busy. The Blue Mountain coffee was the same. Santucci sat down where he could see the door.

CHAPTER 48

Santucci spent the day in the area of the *Caff &
net* since he didn't have anywhere else to go, and
they hadn't found Thistlethorn. Milo knew where he
was; they'd talked a few times. Milo probably felt that
Santucci was in a good place, out of the way.

He talked to Ariano. The Chameleon was in fact
on the DCFS computer network, FBI, ATF, and just
about every other government system Ariano had
checked. Files that were classified and protected by
numerous laws and safeguards were an open book to
whoever had the codes. They were still learning about
the program. Milo and Ariano had talked. Milo had
called his people. One thing they were in agreement
on, Thistlethorn would be needed to clean up the
mess.

Santucci had also told Ariano to put together a car
for Milo's son. A kid's car, but nothing too hot. Didn't
want to make Polly nervous. One thing for sure, the
car that Santucci had borrowed from the kid was a

piece of junk. It needed a new engine and the tie rod was so bad the steering wheel vibrated. Santucci told Ariano to send him a car, too. He parked the little car in a city lot across from the coffee shop and set up an office.

Santucci had canceled a date and also informed Angel Akin that her system had been compromised by Thistlethorn. She seemed relieved and a little sorry that their date was off. Santucci had been having thoughts about Akin that he had never had before. He more than just *liked* her. It was a little scary. He was doing things that seemed foolish and definitely out of character, for Santucci anyway. In Michael's words, he was acting silly. Maybe that was because he hadn't had sex for, for as long as he could remember, must be weeks now. It probably affected the brain.

He was tired of looking at his computer screen in the cramped little car and thought that he would go back into the coffee house and get another cup of the afternoon brew, a Kona Valley bean. If you put enough cream and sugar in the cup they all tasted the same. He was on his tenth cup.

While he was in there, he thought he would use the bathroom, an old style affair that had a few urinals appended to the back wall. When he tried the door, it was locked so he went back to get his coffee. When he returned, he caught a glimpse of a mop of hair going out a rear door of the place. He had noticed that door earlier but hadn't been able to watch it very well. He had looked out there once and had seen a small yard, fenced in, that faced a railroad track.

Santucci wasn't sure why, maybe it was the caffeine, but he ran towards the back door. It was glass with a metal bar across the middle. When he reached it he looked out and didn't see anyone. He went into the little yard and looked towards the front of the building. No one.

Walking to the fence, a four-foot chain link, Santucci leaned over and looked south, down the Illinois Central Line. There he was. And he still had the hair.

Santucci looked around and could only see one direction to go. He jumped the small fence, as Thistlethorn must have done, and landed on the egg-sized rocks that made up the track bed. Thistlethorn turned, a large coffee in hand, saw Santucci and took off, coffee flying.

The young man stumbled for a few steps and then got his feet under him. He moved up to the tracks and started pacing himself along the ties, hitting them in stride. Santucci pulled in behind him. Neither man was running wildly, seemingly to save some strength, and a sort of pace developed.

Santucci noted the young man's stride and realized he was a runner but he wasn't the only one. Santucci thought of his cell phone, back in the little compact car. He looked around. The yards and buildings passed by. In front was the endless track, the rails of which seemed to come together in the distance, but never did. A railroad track ran through a city, but it wasn't part of the city. Nobody paid any attention to it unless they had to stop for a train. There was no train coming from either direction. Santucci plodded on, his feet not quite comfortable with the distance between the ties or with the handmade Italian shoes.

Thistlethorn looked back, saw Santucci still behind him and tried to increase his speed. He almost tripped and settled for the lead he had. Santucci settled, too. He had to keep the kid in sight. He thought of calling out to him, "Stop or I'll shoot!" He saved his breath; he had no gun either.

They were soon out of town. Thick brush and trees lined both sides of the tracks. After about a mile, Thistlethorn looked back again. Santucci pointed his index finger at him and crooked it a couple of times, signaling "Come here." The eyes that looked out of the bearded face and thick mop of hair were afraid now. That was more like it, Santucci thought. He should be afraid. Santucci was not going to quit, period. Was Thistlethorn capable of running him to death?

After another mile Santucci was running out of steam. His usual workout was three miles, but the added stress of running on the tracks was taking its toll. So, to his delight, was it telling on Thistlethorn.

The young man suddenly veered to the left and plunged into the woods.

Santucci leaped after him, renewed by the perceived weakness in his prey. He didn't have far to go. Thistlethorn had tripped and was just getting to his feet when Santucci pounced on him. They rolled around the ground for a bit; the young man thought he was going to fight with Santucci. He didn't get a chance.

Where Santucci was from, there were no rules, just ruthlessness. Santucci grabbed two handfuls of hair and began beating Thistlethorn's head against whatever happened to be under it. The kid stopped moving and Santucci just laid on him for a moment, trying to get his breath. He would have rested longer, but he had had to pee the whole time.

That taken care of, he tied Thistlethorn up with his belt and shoelaces and started to look around for the next thing he needed. A car. Santucci followed the path they were on, realizing that it was one made by four-wheel ATV's and soon came to a parking lot that was surrounded on three sides by apartment buildings.

Santucci picked out a 1995 Toyota Corolla, went around to the passenger side, grabbed the windshield wiper and broke it off. Then he removed the wiper blade and was left holding the long thin arm. Being in the chop shop business had taught him quite a bit. In Japan, a country where the walls were sometimes made of paper, locks were the last thing they paid any attention to.

Santucci went around to the driver's side, slid the wiper arm down between the glass and the door, jiggled it around and the door lock opened. He got in the car, put the seat belt on from habit, inserted the tip of the same metal arm into the ignition and turned. The engine started when he gave it some gas. As an afterthought, he took one of his business cards, wrote on it, "The police have your car," poked the wiper arm through it and tossed it out the window.

Santucci jumped the little car up over the curb and drove it down the wooded path. When he got back to where he had left Thistlethorn, the kid was awake and had struggled to his feet.

"Hey man, are you fucking crazy? What kind of cop are you? If you're gonna arrest me....."

Santucci shot a short right hook to Thistlethorn's chin, which was sticking out indignantly. If you put your shoulder into it, and hit the button just right, only a six to ten inch shot will do the trick, made famous by Joe Louis. Thistlethorn's head snapped back and he crumbled to the ground. Santucci used a few things he found in the car to further secure his package and he was on his way.

He stopped by Milo's kid's car in the lot across from the *Caff & net* and got his phone and laptop. He didn't call anyone. Then he stopped by an auto parts store and bought a few items. Out in the parking lot he opened the trunk of the stolen Toyota. Thistlethorn was coming around. Santucci took a couple of the shop towels he had purchased and saturated them with two over-the-counter products he had also purchased at the auto parts store. Then he put the towels next to the gym bag that Thistlethorn was wearing like a hood.

"Take a nap, Merlin," he said. Then he slammed the trunk lid, jumped in the driver's seat and sped south.

CHAPTER 49

Except for a little road sign, no bigger than a mail box, you can't tell when you're going past the United States Maximum Security Prison in Marion, Illinois. That's not by accident. Over the years of its existence the institution has housed the most dangerous criminals in the world. Many other prison systems are modeled after Marion.

When Santucci pulled the little compact car up to the guardhouse, he pulled over, out of the way, knowing he might be waiting a while. He identified himself to the officer who came out of the shack and asked to speak with the warden in charge.

Assistant Warden Sullivan was the ranking officer in charge and agreed to allow Santucci to come down to the entrance of the SuperMax to discuss something that Santucci would only describe over the phone as a matter of national security.

Santucci bypassed the parking lot the guard had directed him to and drove right down into the valley the prison lay in, right up to the front door. There was a man in a white shirt standing inside the heavy glass of the doorway. Santucci motioned for him to come out to the car. The officer scowled, then looked to the guard inside the control room and was buzzed out.

"Look here, Lieutenant, you can't just drive up here, talking about matters of national security. We've had no calls." The tall thin warden was used to things running smoothly and people not giving him any trouble. He had a surprise coming.

Santucci took out his wallet and removed a leather ID folder from deep inside it. He opened it and handed it to Assistant Warden Sullivan. The officer took his time, looking closely at the photo, then at Santucci, back and forth a couple of times. Only three or four people had ever seen it. Santucci waited patiently.

"You said you were state police."

"I am." Santucci said, not explaining further. He didn't have to and Sullivan knew it.

"Fine." Sullivan was a little exasperated. "What do you want?"

"I have a prisoner in the trunk of this car. He is a domestic terrorist and a national security threat. As I mentioned before, he is being held, incognito, under provisions of the Patriot Act."

"In the trunk?" Sullivan had been leaning over the driver's window like a traffic cop. He looked at the trunk, it was pretty small.

"You can't......." He looked at the ID in his hand. "Oh hell.....what do you want?" He sounded resigned now.

"I want a wheel chair and access to a cell in block 1A."

"1A! Man, there ain't even no power on in that section anymore. 1A was closed by court order." Times had changed, you couldn't confine humans under inhumane conditions. At least the court had said so.

"Give me a flashlight. And I'm in a hurry."

"Sheeeit!" Sullivan was complying but wasn't happy about it. Santucci didn't care. Thistlethorn was going to talk, and fast.

When Sullivan brought the wheelchair he told Santucci that he would not assist him in any way. Neither would any of the personnel of the penitentiary.

"Good." Santucci answered.

Santucci manhandled the still unconscious Thistlethorn into the wheelchair. "Can you get the door?" Santucci asked.

Sullivan noticed the chemical smell coming from the trunk and scowled some more but he went and held the door, motioning for the inside guard to open the subsequent doors into the facility.

Once inside they moved out of that building, past the first boundary of fence and razor wire, into the next building. There they waited until the gigantic section of bullet-proof glass slid back and Santucci pushed the wheel chair into the tunnel, gulping down the panic that started to rise in him.

Hell, he told himself, this had been his idea. The only way into the maximum security section was through this tunnel. It was wide enough to drive a vehicle through. Evenly spaced gun- ports lined both walls. There were also many other surprises unauthorized personnel would face in that tunnel.

They wouldn't be needed today. When the back wall of the tunnel had closed, Santucci continued pushing the chair through the maze of the bowels of the institution, Sullivan motioning for doors to be opened before them. Sullivan realized that Santucci had been there before.

At a turn they came to a steel door that was partially open. On the outside there was a chipped and faded "1A" painted on it.

It was obvious that Sullivan wasn't going any farther. "Don't come and tell me that this guy has become a corpse," he said matter-of-factly.

"Don't worry, this is just for effect," Santucci tried to assure him, even though he didn't have to. There was no need to antagonize these people.

As Sullivan pulled the big door open, it creaked. "If you're looking for effect, this is the place. It even gives me the creeps." Sullivan had relaxed a little when he was informed that he wasn't going to be witness to a homicide. Maybe this would turn out · alright. Nah.

Sullivan pulled the key out of the door and handed it to Santucci who pushed the chair into the dark interior of the cell block. His breath became quicker and his heart sped up noticeably. He chided himself again for coming up with this stupid idea. Thankfully, only a few steps in, someone threw a switch and several of the round overhead lights came on. The heavy door closed behind him with a final metal clang. It was effective.

Thistlethorn started to come around and the next thing the kid realized was that he couldn't move. Santucci took the gym bag off of his head and untied his hands and feet. He was still groggy from the cocktail that Santucci had cooked up for him.

"Merlin....no, don't say anything until I explain your position."

Thistlethorn groaned and looked around. It was apparent that he was afraid.

"You are in a maximum security federal prison. No one knows you're here. No one. The people who work here don't know who you are. And they don't care." He added for emphasis, although from the look on the kid's face much more wouldn't be needed.

"You are going to be in this facility for the rest of your life."

"Please. I don't know what you're talking about. What did I do?" he whispered.

Santucci was puzzled. "Tell me about the disk."

"Oh."

"Yeah. *Oh.* Go on. You didn't commit those murders, but you're going to tell me who did." That was a promise.

"Murders?" he questioned, and received no answer. Thistlethorn looked around at the little cells that lined the tier, each one holding horrible dark memories. "Okay, so I tried to load the program onto your laptop. That's not a crime, is it?"

"That program is on government computers. Federal offense, pally. Who are you working the program for? Who are you supplying the information to? Tell me, or I'm going to lock you in one of those cells and let you think about it for a week or two."

The kid's eyes got bigger. Santucci wasn't kidding and the kid knew it. "I put it on a couple of systems at school. The library. The newspaper. I didn't put it on any government systems. I'm not giving anyone information. I don't know what you're talking about."

"You wrote it?" Santucci said.

Thistlethorn only nodded.

"You loaded it onto the DCFS network?"

"I don't know what you're talking about. What's BCFS?" The boy was matter-of-fact. A shred of doubt began to surface in Santucci. Yet, could this kid be someone really sophisticated? He was too young to be any kind of deep cover operative. He was too soft also.

"Who did you give the program to?"

"A lot of people. For spying on their girlfriend's e-mails and shit. That's all. Twenty-five bucks."

"You sold that program for twenty-five dollars?" Santucci saw him nod again.

"To who?" Santucci could hardly believe this kid. Did he not realize what the program was capable of?

"I don't know, a lot of people."

"Merlin, you better remember and fast. Your future depends on it."

CHAPTER 50

After Santucci had canceled their date, the day had continued to go downhill for Angel Akin. She was beat and looking forward to a hot soak and a frozen spinach soufflé. The only thing good about today was that the Advocate had been silent for another day. Maybe it was over, she prayed. No, it would never be over. Not for her at least.

Her house was on a quiet street, out on the edge of town. When she stopped at the end of her driveway, she didn't notice the pickup truck parked across the street. She got out of her car and was reaching into the mailbox for some letters when she realized that someone was sneaking up behind her.

Having lost the advantage of surprise, her assailant charged her. She only had a split second to react and drop down, letting his momentum carry him over her. Then she rose up just right, sending him flying over her and somersaulting onto his back with a hard thud. It was her ex-husband, Kyle.

"Kyle, you bastard!"

He wasn't listening. When he tried to get to his feet, she kicked him in the solar plexus, hard. He went down again, unable to breath. His mouth just hung open, his eyes bulging.

For a second she was afraid she had stopped his heart. She felt kind of sorry for him. She calmed herself. "Kyle. Stop. Do you hear me?"

He was on his knees holding his stomach. He didn't, couldn't answer.

"You can't hurt me any longer, mentally or physically. It's over. Understand?" She realized she was crouched in a fighting stance. "I've trained hard, studied martial arts, to ensure that you could never hurt me again. I took responsibility for protecting myself, and I can. Do you need me to prove it to you?"

He stayed on his knees. Whatever he had had in mind was forgotten.

When he didn't speak, she went on. "Now this incident is going to be reported to the police. I'm going to file a complaint and there will be a permanent order of protection issued against you. I've had it with you. If it weren't for Susan, I'd break every bone in your body and love every crack. Believe me, you bastard, I've dreamed of doing it a thousand times. This is your last warning. Stay the fuck away from me!" Her voice was menacing.

His eyes filled up with tears. He found his voice and started to say, "Please."

"You don't talk to me!" She pointed at him and stopped his words.

"There's no talking, no nothing between us! Now get your bony ass out of my sight. She made a move toward him, faking a kick and he scrambled away. He got to his feet, wiped his tears, and with one last injured look walked unsteadily across to his truck. She watched him all the way, part of her hoping he would drop that last straw onto the camel's back.

Akin retrieved her mail, got into her car, and pulled it up to the house. Her house was a country-style ranch with a covered porch that ran across the front. When she got out of her car she saw someone sitting in a wicker chair that she had hung from a stout roof beam. It was a man and he was wearing a St. Louis baseball cap. She thought about getting back in her car. She had a lot of options, but this was her house, and she was still pumped up from her encounter with Kyle. She shouldered her bag, her cell phone at hand, and stepped up to the porch.

The man in her favorite chair was Amy Crocker's father, Jack. She felt sorry for him, too; he had a real tragedy. Amy was not responding to treatment. She had already been moved several times because she had nightmares and became hysterical easily. Now she was in a mental treatment facility. The situation was a sad one for Jack Crocker, but that didn't mean that he was welcome at Akin's home.

"Mr. Crocker. I'm sorry but you'll have to excuse me. I can't talk to you right now." She wasn't listening to anything he had to say. Regardless of what he wanted, it could wait until office hours, tomorrow.

"Oh, you can't?" He didn't get up. "Then I'll just tell you not to worry. That I will continue to keep your secret, Doctor."

"What secret?" She didn't have time for games.

"That you were the one who killed Warren Knoop, Doctor." He looked at her knowingly. "That you are the Advocate."

CHAPTER 51

"Yes, Milo, I've got him and we're coming back over to the house. He says that he has the names of everyone that has the program filed in one of those computers. No, he says he's the only one who can access it."

They were on their way north, through the forest, Assistant Warden Sullivan glad to see the back of Santucci and guest.

"You'd better be able to do what you said you could do, Merlin." Santucci looked over at his passenger who seemed to be naturally groggy. "You're either going to be a guest of the government or be working for them for the rest of your life at any rate."

The boy looked over unhappily, the realities of life setting in. "Don't worry, I can fix it." He hoped.

"Open my laptop and access the Callahan file." The young man did as he was told.

Once he had it on the screen, Santucci told him what he wanted. "You said you remember most of the names of the people who you sold the program to. Start checking that file to see if any of them are in it."

"Why would they be in this file?"

"Just do it." Santucci wasn't answering any questions. Thistlethorn started to comply without any further comment.

When they reached the grubby little campus house that Thistlethorn lived in, it was all abuzz. Santucci escorted him into the main room and introduced him to Milo.

"I remember him from that first night," Milo said by way of a hello. He wasn't impressed with Thistlethorn, at least not with the way the kid looked or smelled. "Now sit down and get that list up or you're going to go someplace for a little private conference." Milo was a little strained too. He didn't know where Santucci had just come from.

"Okay, no problem." Thistlethorn had had enough of private conferences to last a lifetime, a lifetime either working for the government or in prison. He was eager to comply.

Santucci had his laptop ready to compare the names Thistlethorn brought up with the list of Callahan's actual and potential victims. After all this time, it was anticlimactic. When Milo called out the name of Jack Crocker he looked over at Santucci. Santucci arrowed down his list to the Cs . There was the name. John R. (Jack) Crocker. He had been a student at the

Catholic elementary school where Father Callahan was the parish priest from 1978 to 1985. Most of the pedophile's attacks had occurred during the late 70's and 80's.

"That guy's a cop," Thistlethorn said, expressing doubt in Crocker's complicity.

"Yeah, he's a cop all right," Milo said with as much scorn as he could generate.

Santucci thought for a moment, then hastily pulled out his phone and made a call. After a few moments he said into the receiver, "Angel, this is Diego. Call me as soon as you can."

He closed his phone and looked at Milo. "Have a car go over to her house. When I met that bounty hunter guy at DCFS that day, I remember the screen on Dr. Akin's computer changing when I walked into her office. Crocker had been in that office for a while before we came. I'll bet he loaded the program onto her laptop."

Santucci was thoughtful again, and worried now. "Forget the car. I'll go over to her house. Send the car for Crocker. Send all the damn cars for Crocker."

He was angry too, with himself. Although he had no reason to be, the clues leading to Crocker had been vague. Santucci remembered Akin contradicting Crocker's opinion of how well his little girl was progressing after being molested by.......McKinney....... Delbert McKinney.

"And Milo, find out where a child molester by the name of Delbert McKinney is right now. That's what all this has all been about. He's going to kill McKinney."

Milo started to move, excited by the prospect of action. For a second he forgot Thistlethorn, who was trying to fade into the woodwork. Milo grabbed him by the shoulder, roughly lifting him to his feet. "You're with me, "Wonderboy," he mocked.

CHAPTER 52

Akin tried not to show how surprised she was. It wasn't very effective.

"Yes, Doctor. I know all about it," Crocker said, a conspiratorial grin on his face.

She stepped onto the porch, closer to her front door, keys in her hand.

He didn't move.

"I don't know what you're talking about. And as I said, Mr. Crocker, I cannot speak with you now. Tomorrow perhaps...."

"Don't you want to know the reason that I'm here?"

She clearly did but tried to continue the ruse. "No," she said, but didn't move any closer to the door.

He smiled now. "You see, when I was checking your e-mail....."

"My e-mail?" She questioned, clearly taken by surprise.

"Oh, yes, Doctor. In fact I have an entire copy of your hard drive. That's how I found out that you were the Advocate."

She was riveted now. She could see he was very proud of himself.

He went on, unable to resist gloating. "People forget how computers work. When you deleted your message from the Advocate, you only deleted the connection that your computer would use to access it. The message stays on your hard drive until something is recorded over it. I retrieved the message before that happened. I *know* you killed Warren Knoop after he tortured and murdered that little girl. I must say that I think it was a noble act. I commend you, Doctor."

She looked at him in a new light. The red baseball cap. Then she had it. She remembered reading Delbert McKinney's name on the list of sex offenders who were going to be released tomorrow.

"Back to the reason for my visit. When I was checking your e-mail, I saw a photo of a checkout station at, what looks like, a Wal-Mart store. I'd like to know more about that picture."

She started for the door. "Mr. Crocker, as I've said before. I don't know what you're talking about and I don't have time to talk to you any longer. If you have information for the police about the Advocate, I suggest you tell them."

He got up from the chair and stepped towards her. "I'm sorry, Doctor, but I can't afford...."

She couldn't, didn't wait any longer. She launched herself at Crocker, striking out for his head and, at the last possible moment, when his guard went up, she went for his knee. The knee blew out. If she could just get away.

He hollered and went down, but he had a hold of her leg. They battled on the porch for what seemed like ages but was actually only seconds. Finally, he caught her in the side of the head, with a meat cleaver fist, and she was out. He lay there for a moment, breathing heavily, assessing his own damage. There was blood streaming down his face where she had apparently gouged him with her keys. He ignored the ringing of a phone that came from Akin's nearby purse.

CHAPTER 53

When Santucci got to her house, and stepped onto the porch, the first thing he saw was blood. He tried to control his panic. The only good thing about it was that it was only a little blood. Drops and smeared blood from wounds received during a fight, for example. Not the kind of blood you'd expect to see if someone had a major injury. He wasn't doing a very good job of calming himself.

Then he spotted Akin's purse. When he found her keys, with blood on them, he prayed that she had been the one to draw blood. He called Milo.

"Milo, Crocker's snatched her. She e-mailed that Wal-mart photo to herself, that has to be it. Get a team over here. I want this whole area gone over. I want a grid search, dogs, horses, ATV's. I want every damn thing that Sheriff Gilbert had and more."

Milo didn't say anything; he knew the situation was grave.

Santucci had another thought. "You said that McKinney is getting out tomorrow? Akin must have figured out that Crocker is the killer, or Crocker may just think she knows. Either way, he thinks he has to keep her out of the way until he kills McKinney. At least." At most, she'd be out of the way permanently.

"Get the numbers on his personal cell phone and start tracking it. I want every chopper available." Santucci was frantic, and he was still driving a stolen car.

Within an hour they had Crocker's cell phone's ESN number and were ready to track it. The only problem was that Crocker didn't have it turned on, and he was nowhere to be found. Santucci spent the night driving around southern Illinois aimlessly. He knew that Milo would call him the second Crocker turned his phone on. He just hoped he was in the right place when it happened, if it happened.

At 6:00 a.m. sharp, Crocker's phone went on and the boards lit up. Milo called Santucci.

"Diego, he's in Saline County. The towers are far apart out there. Do you have a map?"

"I have my laptop. Give me the locations of the towers and get every available car out here."

Santucci was on the edge of the triangular area that the cell phone was transmitting from. The problem was the area was about a hundred square miles. There was one hope. If Crocker was moving and left the radius of one receiver, and was then picked up by another tower, that would give them direction and reduce the search area; but he wasn't moving. Crocker's signal didn't come into any other cell tower.

Crocker's vehicle description had been broadcast all night; Santucci could picture it in his mind. He heard a chopper go over and wished he had his own car, for the millionth time, so he could talk with the chopper pilots and hear the ground unit radio traffic. It seemed hopeless.

Santucci remembered Akin goading him into the church, where the shrine of St. Jude was, that night after tacos and asked the patron saint of hopeless cases for help. He was willing to do anything to save her. His phone rang.

"Milo, tell me something," Santucci clutched the phone like a lifeline.

"Not a lot, Diego," Milo said quickly, not wanting Santucci to get his hopes up. "The call that Crocker made was to the sheriff's office. He asked what time Delbert McKinney was getting out of jail. He said he was McKinney's brother and wanted to pick him up."

"What did they tell him?" Santucci was disappointed but wanted to make sure that the plan, such as it was, was going well.

"They handled it well. They told Crocker that he would be released at 9:00 a.m.

"What about McKinney?" Santucci didn't much care whether they saved the child molester or not, but he had stopped short of letting McKinney go without telling him about Crocker.

"McKinney has asked not to be released. He's going to hide in a nice cozy jail cell until it's all over and he can get back to drugs and pedophilia." Milo was clearly disgusted. "We have a sheriff's deputy who looks pretty much like McKinney and is willing to pose as him. He'll walk out of the jail at 9:00 a.m. sharp and set himself up as bait for Crocker."

Santucci didn't know who the young deputy was, but he was going to find out and thank him. For the time being, he was speeding up and down the back roads of Saline County in a fruitless effort. An hour went by. It was now 7:00 a.m. His phone wasn't ringing; Crocker hadn't moved into the range of another cell tower. He saw a sign that read Mine Road #25. Private. It was as good a sign as any. He turned, the gravel of the seldom used grassy lane shooting out behind the little Toyota.

CHAPTER 54

He had raised a cloud of dust, driven to the end of the road and found only the rusted locked gates of an old coal mine. On his way back he saw a side road that was grown over, but had the grass bent down where a vehicle's tires had passed over it. He took a chance and turned, bouncing down the rutted path.

Another sign, bent over and almost unreadable with age, read; Temple Salt Mine: Property of the State of Illinois. CLOSED; NO HUNTING NO TRESPASSING. The road went down into a small valley and he followed it until he came to a cliff face that had a large irregular hole in the side of it. Crocker's pickup truck was parked under some trees that had enough leaves on them to hide it from the sky. Santucci looked up and said, "Thank you".

Santucci left the Toyota in the clear and called Milo. "I'm at an abandoned salt mine, the Temple Salt Mine. I don't know where the hell I am. Oh! It's somewhere off Mine Road number 25. Get me some back-up quick. Crocker's truck is here."

"Diego, wait until we get some help over there." Milo said uselessly. Santucci had already disconnected.

The opening of the mine was different from the way they dig a modern coal mine with huge drilling machines. This mine was old. It had been worked by hand and closed when salt became a cheap commodity a century earlier. Santucci checked Crocker's truck before he headed for the opening. Empty.

Once more Santucci wished for his car, where there was a flashlight in the glove compartment and a gun, too. The chain-link wire gates that partially covered the opening were not locked. No lock or chain in evidence. He passed the gates, stepped into the darkness, and was immediately overwhelmed by the claustrophobic feeling. He stopped to get his bearings, and to muster up some courage. Then his phone rang, echoing loudly off of the solid crystal walls of the salt cave.

Frustrated, he backed up against a wall and looked at the display. It was Michael. Maybe something was wrong, he worried. Then he thought, what could be more wrong than the situation he was in right now? He answered it anyhow.

"Diego, are you okay?" The boy's voice didn't have any of its normal cheerfulness, not a hint of joy that Santucci loved to hear.

"I'm fine, Michael," Santucci whispered. "I'm busy right now. I'll call you back in a little while, all right?"

"Are you going under the house?"

"Uh............kind of." Santucci didn't have time to wonder how the boy knew this.

"Take your watch off," Michael said, then added, "call me after you catch the bad man." He disconnected without another word.

Santucci looked at his left wrist and saw the soft glow of his Submariner. He stopped, tried to clear his mind, and spent a moment thinking about how to proceed instead of charging ahead as he had started to do. He found a piece of an old two-by-four; his watch fit snugly around one end of it. Carrying the board by the other end he started back down the tunnel.

Once he got down a few hundred feet, it was completely dark. Darker than night. He knew this darkness. He willed his heart to beat slowly and tried to control his breathing. It wasn't working very well.

He moved forward with his ears, trying to remember the drill from the days in Viet Nam. As an afterthought, he took his sunglasses out of his coat pocket and put them on. He heard some noise far down the tunnel.

He wasn't going to surprise Crocker, not after Michael's call. "Jack Crocker!" he called out down the tunnel. He waited and called again. "Jack Crocker!" His voice echoed down into the darkness.

"It's over Crocker, McKinney is not getting out of jail today." He waited.

That changed the plan for Crocker. "Very good, Lieutenant." The voice was close. Only fifteen or twenty yards away Santucci figured.

"Give it up. It's over," Santucci said, hoping to talk him out.

"It's not over until that fiend is dead!" Crocker's voice was anguished. "You will not stop me from killing that monster!"

"Where's Dr. Akin?" Santucci wasn't sure whether he should ask or not, but finally couldn't help himself.

"She's right here, Lieutenant. Come and get her." He had a new plan forming. "She's no use to me now. Is she any use to you, Lieutenant?"

Santucci bit down on his answer. He started moving closer to the voice, holding the board out in front of him.

"Tell you what," Crocker said. "You let me go and I'll give you the good doctor. How 'bout it?"

"Okay," Santucci said with as much assuredness as he could. "Just let her go and you can leave." He moved closer and realized that his head was now brushing the ceiling of the tunnel. Reaching out with his ears, he heard Crocker move. Away.

Crocker was listening too. Neither one of them had any intentions of completing any deals. Crocker had already figured that Santucci was alone. He was placing himself for the assault.

There was no more talking now. They both knew what was going on. Maybe Crocker figured he could avoid capture long enough to kill McKinney, if he could just get past Santucci. His job was finding fugitives; maybe he thought he knew how to be one better than anyone else.

Santucci didn't care. He moved forward, crouching down now. The tunnel narrowed and the ceiling now forced Santucci almost to his knees. He moved the board in front of him and heard a *sprrrring*. Milo's guess of a spike that shot out of a rod with a powerful force was right. Santucci thought he could feel the tip of the spike stop right in front of his face.

Crocker switched on his flashlight, hoping to blind Santucci, but the sunglasses blocked enough of the light for him to see where Crocker was. He dived for the floor and scrambled forward.

Crocker was already on his knees in the tunnel. He tried to pull his weapon back so the point would be in an effective position, but Santucci was already inside his defenses. Santucci grabbed for anything. Crocker dropped the weapon and flashlight, forced to go hand to hand with Santucci.

It all came back for Santucci. He was back in Viet Nam. Fighting for his life in the darkness underground. Crocker was stronger in some ways, but couldn't use the advantage of his longer arms because of the wrestling hold that Santucci had on him.

They fought tooth and nail, literally. Minute movements shifted the advantage back and forth. Finally Crocker had his hands around Santucci's throat and started to exert the superior strength of his arms. Santucci could feel himself losing consciousness.

He remembered Viet Nam, when his buddy Frankie had bought it. When they had pulled Frankie out of the tunnel, his fingers were ripped to shreds and there was a wire around his neck. His face was swollen and purple, and his eyes........his eyes had been torn out. They did finally dig out and kill the Viet Cong officers who were hiding in those tunnels, but how many times could you kill them? You couldn't kill them enough to bring Frankie back.

Santucci realized that the index finger of his right hand was next to Crocker's nose. He didn't hesitate. He forced his finger into Crocker's eye socket. He could feel the eyeball. His finger was behind it now. All he had to do was pluck it out. The tension around his neck lessened and he heard something. Crocker was screaming.

"Let go!" Santucci croaked. The tension lessened but Crocker didn't relinquish the hold he had on Santucci's throat.

"I'll pluck this mother out and eat it!" Santucci wasn't kidding. Crocker let go. Santucci didn't.

"Where is she?" Santucci whispered into Crocker's face, his voice deadly. When there was no immediate answer Santucci moved his finger, just a bit. Crocker screamed again.

"She's in my truck!" he cried.

"She's not in your truck." Santucci prepared to rip Crocker's eye out and start in on the rest of his body.

Crocker felt it. "Please man! She's in my truck. In the tool box."

Santucci remembered the little stainless steel tool box that was mounted in the rear bed of Crocker's pickup truck. You couldn't fit a person into that. He had to take the chance though.

"If she's hurt you'd better find a way to kill yourself before I get back," Santucci said icily. He pulled his finger out of Crocker's head, got up, and started running up the tunnel.

CHAPTER 55

When Santucci reached the mouth of the tunnel, the light did blind him, having lost his sunglasses back in the mine. It took him a second to adjust but he didn't stop running. Finally, stumbling, he found the truck. He jumped up into the back and tore at the latch lock of the tool box. He opened the lid and there was a flash of red hair in the sunlight. She was in there, folded up like a road map.

She didn't move and panic rose up in him. When he touched her she sprang out of the box, like a child's toy, ready to fight, but she had been in there too long, and she was bound hand and foot. She wouldn't have been much of a struggle for Crocker.

When she saw that it was Santucci, tears came into her eyes to match his. He had jumped back when she sprang out and stood in the back of the truck with a stupid grin on his face, crying with joy.

She leaped forward and put her arms over his head and hugged him close. After a second she apparently had time enough for a few other thoughts and released him yelling at him through the duct tape that covered her mouth.

He realized that she was screaming questions at him and cursing up a blue streak at the same time. The tape covering her mouth could wait a moment or two. Santucci untied her feet then reached for her hands and found the end of the tape unwinding it until her hands were free. Then he reached for a corner of the piece covering her mouth. She pushed his hand away and found the corner, prepared to rip the tape off.

"No!" Santucci cautioned. "You'll rip your lips off. Take it easy. Here, let me do it."

He pulled gently at the tape, their eyes locked. It was sort of erotic. When he realized it, he was kind of embarrassed. This was not the time........ When the tape was off she asked quickly, "Did you get him?"

"Yes."

"Did you kill him?"

"No." He couldn't tell if she was disappointed or happy about it.

She put her arms around him again and kissed him. For real. Then she pulled back and looked away sadly.

"What's the matter?" he asked, confused.

"Diego, I have to tell you something. I've wanted to tell you from the first, but I thought that I could......... damn, I don't know!"

"I know," he said. "The Knoop case is closed. There would have been no charges. It's referred to as a *Crime of Passion* sometimes. Justifiable." He shrugged.

"You know?" She was baffled.

Santucci reached into his inside coat pocket and took out a little piece of what looked like rubber. He held it up for her to see.

"What's that?" she asked.

"A model of the heel of your left shoe. From the scene that day." He smiled, pointing at her foot. She was still wearing the work suit she had had on yesterday, and of course, her most comfortable work shoes.

"You knew? All the time?" She couldn't believe it. It was like a huge weight was lifted from her shoulders. "Why didn't you tell me?" She wasn't smiling now.

"Need-to-know," he said. She gave him a gentle punch.

"Diego, you rat." She was smiling.

He was happy. Things seemed to be going well so he took a folded sheaf of papers from the same pocket, opened it up, and showed her the top page.

"What's this?" she asked, looking at the figures and columns.

"These are the results of my medical tests, which I passed with flying colors. And the next page is a letter from a board certified urologist. I am certified ready for action Doctor, unprotected."

She had a look on her face that he hoped to see many times in the future. She was holding the papers now and looked farther into the stack. There were drawings of some kind.

"What are these for?" she asked, trying to get past the moment, for a moment.

"Those are drawings for the new children's center. We thought about using a building that already existed somewhere down here, but finally decided that we should build a new one. Then we can choose a central location and have all the extras that you wanted."

She just looked at him, unable to understand what he was saying for a second. Finally she said, "We?"

"Mickey Doohan wants to be in on the project," Santucci laughed. "In fact, if you name it after his mother, I think he'll pay for the whole thing."

She was laughing too, now, and crying. "What's his mother's name?"

"Mary."

"The Mary Doohan Children's Center it is!" she exclaimed.

It was Santucci's turn to be quiet now and she asked him what was wrong.

"What about Michael?" He asked sheepishly.

"What about Michael?" She didn't wait. "Diego, it's always been about Michael," she said seriously.

"It has?" Now he was confused.

"Of course," she said. "Remember that first day that you brought Michael to our office?"

He only nodded, wondering where this was going. "Diego, on that first day Michael told me that you were going to be his new dad."

"He did?" Santucci was delighted. "Why didn't you tell me?"

"Need-to-know," she said with a wry grin. He grabbed her and hugged her to him. She hugged back.

"How's this for a plan?" she asked. "I'll open the center and you retire, like you've been threatening to do. We adopt Michael and you become a Soccer Dad."

He was wondering if they had Golf Dads, too, but he was happier than he'd ever been.

"I like that plan," he said seriously.

"That's not much of a proposal, but I'll take it," she said.

"Proposal?" he asked, reality setting in.

"We only need one more document on that stack, Santucci." She pointed to the papers that had been laid in the bed of the truck. "A marriage license."

He surrendered and kissed her. And she kissed him back with a kiss that sealed all deals. When he opened his eyes, he saw her deep blue eyes were already open, and they were storming. She broke away.

"SONOFABITCH!" she spat, leaping out of the back of the truck. She hit the ground running. She was a little stiff for the first couple of strides, then picked up graceful speed like a cheetah. Her prey was a hobbling Jack Crocker who had emerged from the cave and was hurrying off in the opposite direction, futilely trying to escape.

Santucci looked up and waved at the helicopter that hovered overhead. The vegetation and terrain were too dense for a landing but Santucci could see that the pilot was on his radio directing units to the scene. For the first time Santucci heard sirens that must have been blaring for a while.

When she was ten feet from Crocker, Akin launched herself into the air and landed in the middle of his back. He went down as if he had been poleaxed. Akin rolled and came to her feet facing Crocker. He tried to lever himself to his feet and she kicked his elbow sending him back down into the dirt, screaming. Then she stood over him, reading him the riot act, accentuating every word with a finger pointed at his head like an ice pick. He just lay there, defeated.

Santucci hoped the units would arrive in time to save Crocker further punishment. They were going to have to work on that "anger management" stuff.

THE END

ABOUT THE AUTHOR

Bill O'Shea began his public service career in 1968 when, as a Chicago Police Cadet, he was assigned to the infamous Democratic National Convention. In the ensuing decades as a Chicago Police Officer he had many adventures, some of which are chronicled in his first novel, THE FOOT POST.

In 1992 Bill moved to southern Illinois with his wife, Susan, and established a detective agency under his private investigator's license. In recent years Bill has been active as a Court Appointed Special Advocate, working with children who find themselves mired in the court system. His experiences as a CASA volunteer moved him to write THE ADVOCATE and create the advocacy project.

Bill is now a relentless advocate for the rights of abused and sexually exploited children and fears that it will be a life long endeavor.

Printed in the United States
55381LVS00001B/100-117

9 781425 928759